THE FEATHER AND THE FALL

SARAH CAELAN

The Feather and the Fall

Paperback edition ISBN: 978-0-6458918-9-8

eBook edition ISBN: 978-1-7644815-0-2

Published by Sarah Caelan

www.sarahcaelan.com

January 2026

This is a work of fiction. Unless otherwise indicated, all the names, characters, businesses, places, events, and incidents in this book are either the product of the author's imagination or used in a fictitious manner. Any resemblance to actual persons, living or dead, or actual events is purely coincidental.

 A catalogue record for this
NATIONAL book is available from the
LIBRARY National Library of Australia
OF AUSTRALIA

Edited by: Lisa de Caux

Cover Design by: Donika Mishineva

Illustrations by: Sarah Caelan

THE
FEATHER
AND THE
FALL

SARAH
CAELAN

Contents

For Mikayla.

Thanks for believing in this story. It was our conversation about it in our office that day that helped push me beyond keeping it to just one nearly-forgotten chapter on my blog. Maybe it would have staying in the 'this would be cool to write' pile otherwise!

We'll be waiting in the fog.

Prologue

The turn of dawn stirred the lamplighters into their daily ritual of extinguishing street lamps all across London, a slow procession of dying flames giving way to a sickly grey light that oozed over London's crooked rooftops. The streets were hushed, the city still holding its breath before the chaos of the coming day. Only the faint whistle of a weary constable on his routine plod carried on the fog, song brittle and reedy, drifting like a ghost between the ribs of the buildings.

Constable Harrow rounded the corner of Arlington Street with a yawn cracking his jaw. His boots scuffed against cobblestone, and he cursed under his breath and bent to inspect it. By now, he was only half-attentive, eager for home and the comfort of thin tea and his bed.

He brushed the scuff on his boot over with his thumb. Sighed. Rose. Stretched out his back until it cracked. He glanced around at the fancy towering townhouses either side of him and continued on, picking up his little tune again.

But this time, the whistle answered back.

Almost.

Harrow paused both his song and his footsteps. Looked around.

The whistling continued.

He furrowed his brows and squinted in the half-dark. He'd not seen another person stirring his whole shift. Rarely did people come out in the predawn – not when it wasn't market day for sellers to be travelling to their stalls.

Harrow turned on the spot. Peered up and down the street. There wasn't a pub house in this area – far too fancy – so it wouldn't be a drunk just waking up from crashing in an alley. And this whistling was far too *good* to be a drunk.

If a little haunting.

A self-condescending smile quirked at his lips. He was going crazy, wasn't he? It was dawnlight, so someone was bound to be up and about. Ghosts didn't just walk the streets. It was the tail end of his rotation getting to him. He just needed to keep going, get to the station, switch over. Then he could go home and get to bed.

No more dark thoughts about haunting whistling.

He stepped forward again. Let his eyes roam over the metal numbers on the fancy wrought-iron gates.

Sixteen ... Fourteen ... Twelve ...

Harrow paused again.

Stared through the gaps in the black wrought-iron gate of number twelve.

Three small bodies in white nightgowns lay crumpled like broken dolls in the pristine garden ahead of him. Their limbs were twisted unnaturally, ringletted yellow curls splayed about them, broken necks forcing their faces skyward.

Bare feet stained with earth and blood.

And in the weak morning light, their frozen smiles looked almost holy.

Harrow's exhale shuddered, and a chill prickled at the back of his neck.

The whistling had stopped, and the silence near broke him.

He staggered back, eyes crawling up the façade of the townhouse to the gaping third-story window thrown open above. Lace curtains fluttered innocently in the light breeze. He stepped forward. Checked the garden. No footprints. No ladder. No sign of forced entry.

Only a single white feather caught on the gate's handle, trembling.

1

The Smiles Beneath the Window

Devitt

'Murder on Arlington Street! Read all about it!' cried the newsboys two days later, paper bundles under arms and soot on their cheeks. 'Three young heirs dead in the night!'

Devitt shoved a coin into a newsboy's grimy hand. He crammed the rolled paper into his coat pocket and stalked towards the police station, ignoring the early morning fog curling around his boots like vines. Inside, he grunted at the greeting from Reed – bright-faced, always too cheerful, dashing about like she believed there was still hope – and took the creaking stairs two at a time to his office.

Well, as much as you could call it that.

Cramped, stale, with a paper-strewn desk. It was closer to being called a storage room, with a cracked, grime-smeared window letting in more cold than light.

Devitt slammed the paper on his desk and flattened it with a scarred hand.

'Suspect? Hah.'

He sniffed. The print screamed murder. With theories spun like webs with hints of culprits and drama and everything the media sucked up. But the reality was very different.

Rubbing his face, Devitt dropped into his chair with a groan. He'd not been home in two days. Too much pressure from the top. Martha would be furious. The kids—

He swallowed that thought.

No rest. No clues. Nothing to bring them closer to the answers of this mystery, despite what the papers said. All he had was the disturbing memory from his visit to the scene. Those children's faces – smiling, beatific, as though they'd glimpsed some idyllic dream right before they'd shattered on the stones of their own front courtyard.

There was a knock and a squeaking of shoes in his doorway. 'Detective!'

Devitt didn't look up.

'What do you want, Chattoway?'

The man slithered in. 'Just a friendly check-in,' Chattoway said, stroking his ink-stained fingers together as if he were afraid to touch anything in Devitt's old, dank office. 'The public has a right to know, after all.'

'You mean like all this nonsense you already garbled to the media here?' Devitt gestured to the paper on his desk and revelled in Chattoway's discomfort.

Public relations officer, he called himself. In practice? A meddler who talked too much, too soon, letting the media into every corner of an investigation.

The man shook his head. 'We need to do better. This is a high-visibility case.' And then Chattoway sighed and stared right at him. 'The press mustn't know more than you, Devitt. Embarrassing, isn't it?'

Devitt fought back the urge to bite back. Chattoway was always like this.

'And,' the man continued, avoiding the discomfort, 'You'll be thrilled to hear – the mayor wants a word.'

Devitt's mouth dropped open, and Chattoway grinned. In the way that made Devitt now thoroughly regret not biting back a moment ago. Would've felt better, at least.

'Brush yourself up, man. Wouldn't want to scare the politicians, now, would we? We need them on side.'

The mayor's office smelt of polished wood and overly strong perfume. Everything was so neat and clean in its place that Devitt felt like a stain merely to be there. He stood until the secretary gestured him to a chair.

He sat. Reluctantly.

He wasn't alone.

The mayor paced from behind his desk. Trying to look imposing or important, maybe. But that was impossible with the other guest present.

Beechworth – one of the most prominent politicians of the time and father of the three deceased children – was sitting in the second guest chair just inches away from Devitt, and staring right at him. The politician folded one leg neatly over the other and brushed down his trouser leg with his hand, before lacing his fingers together over his knee.

Devitt's chest spiked.

The man's suit was immaculate, his hair brushed back and oiled with unnatural precision. He looked like a painting, not a man made of flesh and blood and flaws like Devitt and all the rest of London.

'Detective Inspector Devitt,' Beechworth said, his voice like ice scraping over metal. 'Found the killer of my children, yet?'

Devitt clenched his jaw. 'No, sir.'

Was it even worth trying to explain how it was impossible to find an unknown killer in such a short time? Mere days? If someone hadn't been found leaning over with a bloodied knife and a frenzied grin and arrested at the time?

And in reality, that so rarely happened.

Instead, Devitt sat in the awkward silence that followed for far too long, ignoring the exhaustion clawing into the pits of his eyes and the burning of his face with an embarrassment he should no longer feel at his age and level.

But Beechworth's stony glare made it impossible. And the ticking of the old grandfather clock at the side of the room only grew louder and louder until it scraped at Devitt's nerves.

Finally ...

Beechworth leant forwards. Laced his long fingers around his teacup with a restrained grace. 'Pity. I hoped for more.'

Devitt's pulse stuttered, and an urge to defend himself bubbled up. Instead, the mayor interjected, smoothing things over with Beechworth with politics and platitudes and promises the detective knew he'd not be able to keep. But what more could Devitt say when visions of Beechworth's children still haunted his memory.

Their broken limbs. Their smiles ...

'We believe the intruder entered through the third-story window,' Devitt interrupted the mayor.

Both other men turned to look at him.

'No sign of tampering,' Devitt continued. 'No trace of how they got up. Or down. It's as if they flew.'

Something tightened in Beechworth's already stony gaze. 'So you believe in magic, do you, now, Detective?'

Devitt let out a controlled exhale. Of course he didn't. But these were the mysteries that were making the case harder to solve.

But that wouldn't matter to Beechworth. All the man would want was to hear that the killer of his children had been found. Of course it was. Devitt thought of his daughter. And his toddler son. If it were him in Beechworth's place ...

Beechworth sighed and rose. Walked to the window behind the mayor's chair and stared out over the city. 'This was a message.' The man spread his arms wide on the windowsill as if claiming space. 'I'm to be elected prime minister in mere weeks. Someone is making a statement.'

He turned and pinned a glare on Devitt. 'You'll attend tomorrow's electoral party. Keep my wife safe. If you can't bring back my children, then at least protect what I do have left.'

'Excellent,' the mayor turned and nodded before Devitt could even respond. 'That can certainly be done. Can't it, Devitt?' The mayor's eyes bore into his. 'No doubt Scotland Yard is more than capable of such a task.'

Beechworth gave a final thin-lipped smile. 'So it is done. And do find out how they got in. Don't disappoint me again.'

Back on the street, Devitt paused. Let out a long exhale and rubbed at his face. He was hopeless with politicians and official types. This was why they had public relations officers. To let the detectives do their work without all the fake promises.

'Damn Chattoway.' The man should have blocked that meeting. Or gone in Devitt's stead. Devitt wasn't suited to polished rooms and white shirts. Not when his brain was clouded with too many questions about smiling, broken children and a house that wasn't broken into.

He lit a cigarette with shaking hands and stomped back to the station. An almost permanent fog curled through the streets like smoke. Devitt always thought the city felt like it was hiding something. But this morning, it felt like something was watching.

Too damn tense.

It was the case. Of course it was. Setting his nerves on fire.

He focused on what he could control. Rechecking notes. Requestioning the nanny. Rereading the garden inspection.

His eyes glazed over something drawn in chalk on the bricks near the station door. A circle of stars and a smile in the centre.

Childlike. Innocent.

And far too familiar.

2

The Feather on the Gate

Devitt

Devitt reread the case notes over a sad meat pie – more potatoes and watercress than meat. Still, it brought warmth back despite the chill seeping through his cracked office window.

He leant back in his creaking chair. There must be something in these notes that gave some kind of clue. But no matter how often he read them, they still all suggested the children had merely jumped from their own window.

Unprompted. Together.

But had they been unhappy enough to do so, why would they have been smiling?

A dare?

He sighed and rubbed his hand down his face. This was getting nowhere. Something at the scene must have been missed.

Devitt rose with a groan and pulled his coat closer to him, hollering for the assistant Reed as he shuffled down the steps. He asked her to hail a cab and join him. A fresh pair of eyes might do him good, and she was always eager and energetic. Might see something everyone else tired of this world had missed.

They stopped by the local station to collect Constable Harrow, who'd found the children on his dawn plod. Expectedly shaken, Harrow said nothing until the horses were called to a stop outside the townhouse on Arlington Street. Harrow was the first to stumble from the carriage onto the cobblestones, staring at the gate as Reed and Devitt followed.

'Feather's gone,' the constable mumbled.

Devitt followed the man's gaze.

'The bird's feather, you mean?' Devitt asked.

He'd read in Harrow's report about there being a feather on the gate that morning, but it hadn't seemed anything of note.

Even so, he gave the wrought-iron gate a glance over before he pushed through it.

It swung open without a sound.

Devitt almost wished it had creaked. Everything down this street was too quiet – no one stirred, left their homes. Even the horse waiting at the carriage seemed to have sensed something and stood stock still without a huff.

It etched at Devitt's nerves.

He paused on the footpath outside the townhouse, eyes locked on the area where the three dead children had been. By now of course they were in the mortuary, but he could still picture their twisted, broken bodies as if they were lying there in front of him now.

Those unsettling smiles on their faces.

Devitt flinched as the front door to the house suddenly swung open, and tried to put on his best calming smile as he turned to greet the nanny in the doorway. He let his eyes wash over the front of the townhouse again – still nothing concerning to suggest someone had broken in or climbed up – and strode the final few steps to the house.

'Morning, miss,' he said, tipping his hat. 'Here for another look, if you will. I spoke with Mr Beechworth this morning.'

The nanny's face was gaunt, and her eyes shadowed and heavy with no sign she wanted to entertain politenesses. But Devitt was used to that. No one ever wanted to speak with the police.

He gave a nod as he swept the grounds again, taking his time now. Crouching close and stroking the soil. Fingers brushing stone.

What had he missed? Surely there had to be something.

Reed was standing next to the maid, asking questions in hushed tones. About the children. Whether they'd said anything odd in the days leading up to the tragedy. Were there any strange noises from the room that night?

'Nothing.' The nanny's voice cracked, and Devitt turned to see Reed stroking the nanny's back as the maid pulled out a handkerchief and blew into it loudly. Brushed back tears with the corners of the cloth. 'They were such good children.'

'I'm sure they were,' Reed replied sympathetically.

Devitt returned to looking up at the wall outside the children's third-storey window. A pale white curtain blew softly out of it, light as a feather.

'They'd grown increasingly fond of stories and music.' The nanny's voice was quiet. High-pitched from emotion. Devitt let it wash over him as he worked, but doubted there'd be anything else that could help him now. All the main questions had been gone over and over. 'Always talking about adventures. A boy with a pipe. Stories of pirates and mermaids. They were so excited about it. Always drawing. Always humming a tune together.'

Devitt chuckled. Children's fancies. His daughter often got stuck on certain interests for such a long time too. Her current joys were street games like running with her hoop and stick. Next? They grew so quickly it was hard to tell.

His gut sank at the guilt of not going back to see his family for so long, but with the pressure of a high-level politician's family being killed, it was hard to go home.

He needed to solve this as soon as possible. Go home. See Martha and the kids.

But as he glanced back at where Reed stood listening to the nanny – still talking of stars, music, and magical stories – he wasn't sure how much of her talk about daydreams and the perfect children would help him at all.

Reed

The nanny was still talking, but Reed's heart stuttered.

Chalk stars and a boy with a pipe?

She stared, willing the woman to keep talking. To say something else. But, instead, the nanny smiled and sniffed and told the same stories again.

Such good children. Always got ready quickly and calmly before bed, before telling each other stories. Always smiling.

Reed tried to watch the woman. Tried to smile and listen and be encouraging. But inside?

She took a breath. Nodded along as the woman spoke of drawings again. Her heart spiked again.

'Can we see any of these drawings?' Reed asked the woman. And from the corner of her eye, she saw the detective glance up at her from where he crouched under the window. Saw the roll of his eyes as if she wasn't thinking straight.

Ignored it.

The nanny nodded. Said she could fetch some of their drawings from inside.

The detective rose.

'Actually, may we come inside with you? See the children's nursery again.'

The nanny gave a small nod. Turned and led the way inside the house. Reed let the detective and the constable walk ahead of her – expected of her lack of rank – and followed, letting her eyes roam the house. Perhaps she'd see something useful.

Except the house was too clean and too quiet. Just like the rest of this damn street. It was as if the house's soul had been stripped away. It was hard to believe anyone lived here. No sign children had been in the house at all.

Until they got to the nursery on the third floor.

Three beds. Toys lined up on cabinets. Even a change of clothes lay neatly on each child's bed, as if the nanny was still hoping they'd come home.

It was as if someone in their mourning had spent too much time here and tidied things away to clean their own soul too.

The nanny, Reed thought.

And she gave a soft sigh. Nothing for them to see inside the room for any hope of clues, if everything had been tidied away.

The nanny shuffled back with a pile of papers she'd pulled from inside a toy box. Passed them around.

'Even on the walls,' she muttered. 'Naughty children.'

Reed and the other two looked at where the nanny gestured to the wall. Told them she'd been trying to scrub it away, but the children had pressed too hard into the wallpaper.

'Must've been little Mikey,' she said with a soft laugh. 'Always was a bit rough with his pencils. Still learning to control it.'

Reed stared at the mark on the wall. Forgot the papers in her hand. Barely paid attention to whatever the detective was asking the nanny now. Instead, all she could focus on was the ghost of the drawing carved into the wallpaper.

Her heart pounded in her ears.

A moon. Two stars. The second circled.

Surely not. It was nonsense. Children's games. They were the children of politicians. High-ups. Not ...

But she'd seen that shape before. In places that weren't places like this.

A cough in the room brought her attention back. She startled and looked down at the paper in her hands. A pirate ship, perhaps. But the others were talking about music now.

Constable Harrow mentioned he'd heard music that night, too. He'd been humming to himself on his plod, but then a higher-pitched tune had cut over the top and startled him. He'd assumed it was some drunk, though he'd not seen anyone on the street. Perhaps he'd just been getting spooked.

'Nothing to be concerned with,' Harrow said faintly. And Reed wondered how often he'd been telling himself that since. 'Except ...'

She hated the silence that followed. Fiddled with the papers in her hands, watching him, begging him to finish his sentence. You can't say something like that and not finish it.

But the man's eyes looked like they were reaching for something in fog. Something forgotten – almost.

'... I still can't get it out of my head,' he finally said. 'The tune, I mean.' And then his eyes flickered to each of them in turn. 'And what I saw.'

Devitt

Devitt watched the nanny's polite smile wane, and her eyes widened at Harrow's mention of the tune.

'Yes,' she whispered. Folded her hands over her skirt. 'Well ...'

The young woman sniffed again and dabbed her eyes with her handkerchief. Turned her head to look back at the door to the children's nursery.

'I think,' Devitt said, 'it's time for us to head back to the station.' He turned and nodded to the others. Raised his brows. 'Thank you, miss, for your time and additional assistance.'

The nanny smiled gratefully from behind her handkerchief. Spun around far too quickly and quickstepped down the stairs to the front door. Then, before Devitt could even give polite reassurances, she paused at the doorway halfway through shutting the front door.

'Please, detective,' she said, her voice cracking again. Her pale grey eyes flickered up to meet his. 'Please, find out who did this to them.'

And then she shut the door, but not before a faint sob escaped through the final crack.

Devitt looked back at it for a moment before turning to meet the gazes of the others with a sigh. Harrow looked as haunted as ever – near ready to flee – and even Reed was lost in her own thoughts, no longer bouncing around on her feet.

'Let's get back,' he said, hearing the gravel in his own voice, and he adjusted his hat before he strode down the front path back towards the waiting cab. 'Lots to get on with.'

The young woman bound instantly into action, darting down the path past him and holding the gate open for both him and the half-gone ghost of a constable behind him, who then tipped his hat, and with a bare whisper of a goodbye, trudged back to his local station.

'There must be something new we've learnt today that can help,' Devitt muttered, stepping up onto the horse-drawn carriage and then pausing to glance back at Reed as she shut the gate behind them.

She seemed far too young for this job, and he'd never worked with an assistant before. Others in the station called her *young but capable*. Devitt hoped they were right.

But when she didn't join him in the carriage, he peered out again. She was still standing by the gate, staring at the wall.

'Reed,' he said with a warning. 'Time to go.'

She jolted. Turned. Bound back to the carriage with far more speed than necessary. And as she brushed past him, Devitt noticed what she'd been staring at.

Chalk stars on the red brick wall next to the gate. The second one circled.

Devitt clicked his tongue. 'Man told us there was a feather on the gate. Didn't even think to mention the drawings on the wall beside it.' He glanced over at Reed. 'Strange what different people notice, eh?'

The young assistant gave a stiff nod. Turned to stare out of the window as the driver clicked the horse forward.

'Dawn fog plays tricks on you,' she said, but her voice seemed too even. Like someone reciting something they'd said a hundred times before.

But Devitt didn't press. He was too tired for that now. But later, he'd think about how white her knuckles had gone on the carriage door before she shut it for him, and wonder why children's drawings would pull such a reaction from someone.

Or feathers on gates.

'That it does,' he muttered.

3

Stars on a Page

Reed

C halk stars, feathers, and that lilting flute lullaby on the wind?

It couldn't be.

That had been years ago, and it had all gone silent since. A whole other life had passed since Reed had last heard those songs.

It had to be a coincidence.

Except... she thought about it as she strode through the streets, burning off restless energy and the weight in her chest after the Beechworth house visit. And as she did, she reminded herself: in life and death crime, rarely were there coincidences.

Children died every day. Nothing unusual about that. But like this? With smiles on their faces? Jumping, barefoot, from their own windows?

Not with the same drawings each time.

And the music. That tune that Harrow had been humming under his breath. No doubt he didn't even realise it half the time.

Reed clenched her jaw. That sort of stuff didn't happen every day.

Not even in London.

She spun on her heel and marched back to the station.

They'd had reports. A few child deaths over the last few months. Nothing high profile. Easy to overlook, and written off as sleepwalking, illness, rage. All the usual. But there had to be patterns. Something was off.

And Reed would know. As the lowest-ranked, youngest woman in a man's force, she was given all the tedious, menial tasks they didn't want. Like paperwork, filing, closing statements.

Which meant she also knew everything that happened and where everything was. Read reports no one expected her to read. Knew things no one thought she should.

She stormed into the station, boots scuffing the dusty floorboards. Constables looked up, rolled their eyes, muttered behind her back. She knew what they thought: too young, too eager. Always said she'd be crushed by the job eventually.

Let them think it.

She dropped into her rickety desk chair and leant at the necessary angle so it didn't collapse. There were countless handwritten notes in a pile on her desk – she'd intended to look at them today, before the detective called her out. All the child deaths in this area of London going back months. Maybe even years.

The window near her desk was far too murky, barely letting any light in. Here, in the corner of the office, she relied on the lamps she lit.

Someone nearby lit a pipe, and smoke curled across her vision. Reed waved it away and picked up the first report.

Father's violence. No mystery there.

Next – possible illness. Lacerations in the throat from coughing. Damp house. Nothing more.

But the next …

A child from an upper-class family. Fell from a bedroom window in their nightgown. Smiling. Declared sleepwalking. No sign of struggle. Case closed.

Except now they'd seen another.

Three, in fact.

Same smiles, same fall.

Case reopened.

Devitt

Upstairs, Devitt slumped at his desk. He'd gone straight up after Reed had sent the cab away. She'd said she needed to walk. Clear her head.

He didn't blame her.

He'd poured a drink. Something cheap and sharp and that burnt just enough.

The chalk stars. The nanny's stories. Reed had lingered on that wall drawing. Of course he'd noticed. And something about it had stung her. Now he wanted to know why.

Because children drew stars all the time, didn't they?

He pulled a fresh sheet of paper towards him. Began to write:

> *Martha,*
> *Tell the kids I—*

He paused.

The guilt of not going home pressed heavily into his chest, but Beechworth's warning ... The pressure and expectations from all around him ... He felt like he had no choice until this was solved.

Downstairs, he heard the quick boot steps that no doubt sounded Reed's return. No one else walked with that same energy she did. Part of him envied it. Another part of him pitied it. She'd lose it eventually.

Devitt looked back at the letter. He couldn't for the life of him figure out what to tell his wife or kids.

Sorry for not being there? Again?

The tune Harrow had hummed echoed in his skull. It was gentle, infectious. Familiar in a way that he hated. And near impossible to ban.

He wiped a hand over his face and then looked back down at his paper, determined to finish this and send a messenger to deliver it for him.

He stared.

In the corner of the page, drawn without realising, was a star. Five crooked points.

Devitt frowned. Pushed the paper away.

Maybe he needed a walk after all.

4

Leafing Through the Lost

Devitt

A report slapped onto Devitt's desk, jolting him.

Devitt shifted his hand to cover the paper he'd just scribbled on, but not before he noticed Reed had caught sight of the small five-pointed star in the corner.

But she said nothing. Maybe the chalk stars bothered him more than he liked to admit.

'What's this?' he asked, voice rough.

He rubbed a hand down his face and picked up the report.

'Case from a few weeks back.'

Devitt frowned up at her. 'It says it was closed.'

She gestured with her hand for him to keep reading, and Devitt squinted at the handwriting in the dim light.

'Sleepwalking?'

Reed shrugged, but her eyes were firm. 'I think it's oddly similar to the Beechworth case,' she said.

Devitt sighed. Narrowed his gaze as he looked at it again. Certainly, now that he looked at it closely, some elements seemed to match.

'Where did you find this?'

Reed looked behind her and nodded down the steps towards the floor she worked on.

'The cabinets behind my desk,' she said. When she looked back at him, she gave a nonchalant tilt of a dark brow and another soft shrug. 'I'm the one they give all this mess to sort out. I remembered. Went looking.'

She paused. Smirked.

'Found it.'

The line etched deeper into Devitt's brow, and he grunted at the report in his hands. Flicked through the few pages as Reed stood to attention, waiting. The silence as she waited was chilling.

A child falling from their bedroom window during a sleepwalking fit.

Devitt cocked his head. Held out the report for her to take back. 'You got any more like these in those cabinets of yours?'

Reed scowled at him. Snatched the paper back anyway.

'Not my cabinets,' she grumbled, but turned and led the way.

Reed

There wasn't much space at her desk on a normal day, when it was just her tiny body squished between the cabinets at a single-person wooden desk closer to a crate than a piece of furniture. But with the detective stooped there too?

It reminded her of how little she'd been provided for here, the space better suited to a coat rack.

But still, it was a start. Her way in, and she wouldn't complain.

Instead, she gave the detective her chair – trying not to snort when he didn't get the angle correct and nearly collapsed upon sitting – and instead stood by the cabinets, leafing through the papers and passing them to Devitt.

After a small while of working in silence, save for the occasional small mutterings of queries to one another, four cases stood out.

All the same shape as the Beechworths'.

Windows.

Nightgowns.

Talk of children being obsessed with singing hushed lullabies and drawing stars. Speaking of daydreams. Things the police teams would have noted but written down as families reminiscing about things children always do.

A trend that would have been impossible to notice had someone high-up enough not shouted about it.

Reed was mid-grumble to herself about the unfairness of class life when the detective stirred.

'Funny thing,' Devitt breathed out in a whisper, 'how they all smile.'

She glanced over to where the detective had flattened the four reports out on her small desk, all open on the illustrator's sketch of the late child.

Devitt ran his hand over them to smooth them out and leant over to peer closer.

'Eerie,' he said. And then straightened up to look at her. 'When they're all next to one another like this. But alone, nothing to note.'

Reed sighed. Put down the file she'd been scanning. Stared at the four illustrations lying side by side.

Ice shuddered down her spine. Numbed her blood.

'It's not the first time,' she said, her voice barely escaping as a croak. A lump blocked her words. '... that I've seen that.'

Devitt

Devitt looked across the table at her, a wary curiosity digging into his ribs.

'What do you mean?' he prompted when she said nothing, just stared down at the drawings.

Reed looked up – awkward or unsure, Devitt thought. Or both. She glanced around them as if checking it was safe, and then gave a small shrug and cocked her head to the side.

'When I was on the streets,' she said quietly. 'Years back ... When I was a kid ...'

Devitt stared. Felt like some part of his world had been swept from underneath him. As he stared at this young woman now, he couldn't imagine that having been her origin.

'There were chalk stars then too,' Reed continued. 'Same shape. Just kids playing, we thought. Maybe marking territory.'

She paused, leaning back against a cabinet.

'And music too. Humming. Whistling.' She looked up. Met his gaze. 'Pipes.'

The world around them felt too quiet. Beyond these cabinets was an office of constables, Devitt knew. But somehow, this tiny space seemed far bigger and much more isolated.

'There were stories of things happening,' Reed said. 'Thought it was just ghost stories. Kids trying to scare each other. Or turf fights. Or maybe drunks.'

What was? A part of Devitt couldn't wait for her next breath. Begged her to speak faster, though the logic in him knew looking back there must be painful. Things long forgotten. On purpose.

Reed rubbed her temples and squeezed her eyes shut a moment.

'Two kids vanished from where we slept. Just a feather left behind.' When she opened her eyes again, there was a dreamy look. Searching memories, perhaps. 'I thought I imagined the music.' She swallowed. 'Now I'm not so sure.'

Devitt leant back in the chair, lost in thought. It nearly collapsed under him.

He steadied it and gave a quiet huff. 'You need a new chair.'

And then he stared back down at the illustrations. The children's smiles etched into his soul. He templed his fingers and rested his chin on them. 'You ever report it? Any of you?'

Reed scoffed and tossed her head. 'Why would we?'

Devitt looked up at her. Raised a brow to nudge her on.

'No one would've cared. No one cared for kids like us.'

Reed

What could Devitt say to that? He had nothing. And Reed knew it. His blank stare and fish-like mouth said it all.

Even he didn't think of street kids. Of course he didn't. No one did.

But his awkward pause grated at her, and she wished something would happen now to move things on. She shuffled on her feet. Racked her brain to think of something relevant to the case they could talk about. Something safer. More practical.

Instead, the silence and the cramped room brought her world in on her, and half-unlocked memories of the past threatened to break forth.

She tried to push it all away. The old sights, sounds, feelings. Huddling together in the cold. Begging for coin, for food. Damp stone seeping through thin woollen clothes that scratched and itched.

Reed rolled her back as if she could feel it all now. Bid it away. She wasn't there any more. Until—

'There was a name,' she breathed. How could she have forgotten? She glanced over at Devitt who'd blinked and focused on her again. 'Pan. A boy everyone spoke about. Obsessed with faerie circles. Drew stars to mark his territory. Killed birds for fun.' She curled her lips at the thought. 'People said he thought he could summon things with their bones. Or go somewhere else.'

Devitt's lip had curled. Reed got it. She didn't understand the boy's logic either. But there was something else ...

'Said he'd take some of us street kids with him,' she added. Then she shuddered and looked up, as if a fog inside her had cleared. 'Apparently. I never met him. But others whispered about it. I just thought it was fancies. Things to reassure one another on cold or dangerous nights.'

The detective gave a slow, understanding nod and a hum. That much made sense. She'd told herself it over and over anyway.

'And do you know where this boy can be found?'

Reed looked up at the dark ceiling. Tried to remember. 'If it's the same person, he's not a boy any more. But back then, they said he came from St Jude's.'

'The orphanage?'

Reed nodded. Leant backwards against a cabinet and shoved her hands into her too-big coat's overly long sleeves. 'Lucky boy had a bed and all.' She stared at the sleeve cuffs so she didn't have to look anywhere else when she muttered, 'Why'd he have to go bothering us on the streets when he had a room and a bed?'

A long sigh came from where Devitt sat before the chair scraped back and he rose. She looked up. He was staring towards the doorway now – towards the outside. 'People often don't realise what they have. Like to bully those with less.'

And then the detective shoved on his hat. Nodded briefly.

'Come on,' he said. Looked at her. Reed thought his pale green eyes looked clearer than ever. As if he'd finally sorted something out in his head. 'Let's visit the orphanage. See what they know about this *Pan* you mentioned.'

Reed couldn't help her brows rising so high on her forehead she thought she'd have creases for days. She'd just spat out street kid nonsense – stuff adults would normally wave away – and he'd taken it seriously.

No arguments. No jokes.

She pushed herself off the cabinets. Rolled up her sleeves. Gave a single nod back.

This, finally … maybe they could help the street kids after all.

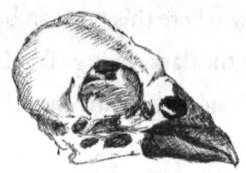

30

5

The Boy at St Jude's

Devitt

Devitt dug his hands into his overcoat pockets, protecting them from the mid-afternoon chill. Reed was marching on ahead, weaving through the crowd easily. She'd not said anything since they left the station, and while Devitt was sure she probably didn't want to say more than she already had, Devitt's head burnt with questions.

He quickened his steps to catch up with her.

'So,' he said, trying to keep casual. 'The streets?'

The young woman glanced back at him but said nothing for a moment.

'When I was twelve,' she said finally, 'there was a fire.'

Devitt's heart lurched. That was enough to know what came next.

Reed dodged a street urchin slipping past with all the ease of someone who knew they were there and how they moved.

'House burnt. Parents were stuck inside.' She paused. 'I was playing games out on the streets with a friend at the time. Saw the smoke.'

She slowed slightly, stepping over a pothole without looking, and then turned to wait for Devitt to catch up.

'I was carted off to my aunty's house, but she had enough on her plate,' Reed continued. Her voice was steadier now. Perhaps too much so. 'Had kids of her own. Didn't need an extra mouth to feed.'

Devitt caught her glancing up at him with a wariness he could finally understand. Clearly judging whether to tell him her story.

'One night,' she said, 'my uncle got drunk. Decided to make me *earn* my stay.'

She raised her eyebrows and shot him a suggestive stare. Careful. Hoping for him to fill in the rest so she didn't need to say it aloud.

Devitt got it. And he hated it.

He stopped walking.

'You were *twelve*?' he asked, hardly able to believe it. Not her, but that someone had the nerve to do that to a child.

'Twelve,' she repeated flatly. Like the word didn't belong to her any more.

She sighed and turned. Kept walking down the grey London streets.

'He failed,' she added when Devitt caught up again, this time able to walk side by side down a less busy, wider street. 'I managed to kick him away, and he was drunk enough it actually worked. So I ran. Thought the streets were safer.'

Devitt frowned, his gaze roaming the streets unseeing. How could he react to that when everything inside him stirred uncomfortably?

Twelve …

He thought of his daughter. A similar age now to Reed then. Imagined someone trying that to her.

Just a child.

Of course he saw enough of that on the force, but to really process it from the mindset of knowing someone. Imagining if it had been his daughter.

He just couldn't.

'I don't know Pan.' Reed's voice cut through his shock. 'But we've all heard of him. Thought it was all an act just to scare us. But the chalk stars and pipe music … It's stuck on the edge of my memory. Things we all saw.' She looked up at him again, eyes sharp. 'But you have to understand that these were all things we just thought were normal. We knew nothing else. But stories and stars and feathers and disappearances … That certainly all happened.'

Finally, they turned a corner, and St Jude's orphanage loomed at the end of the street. Mildew-smothered, hunched, and half-forgotten, crouched on dead ground behind stone walls and iron bars tall enough to pierce the sky. Why such tall bars were needed for children, Devitt couldn't understand.

Utterly rusted through, they looked like they'd been trying to keep something in.

'Not that the bars ever stopped Pan,' Reed muttered.

She stuffed her hands in the pockets of her oversized coat, and Devitt only noticed now how tiny and childlike this giant coat made her look. Wondered how no one had found a better size for her.

'Or any of the others,' Reed added as she stepped forwards. 'They all snuck out. Fought us street kids. Stole things. Then got dragged back like nothing had happened.'

She pushed through the rusted gate.

Devitt lingered, glancing up at the dirt-caked stone slab beside it: *St Jude's Asylum for Boys*, etched deep into the stone. Even the name chilled him – the place for lost causes. Swallowing hard, Devitt pulled the gate shut after them, but it refused to catch. So he gave up.

If the kids escaped anyway, what use was a gate?

Reed

The orphanage towered over them. Grey stone walls had gone black and green in most places with damp and age, with windows too fogged and grimy to see through.

Typical of anything for the lower classes, Reed thought. Nothing clean or new.

But at least they had a roof. And beds, she reminded herself.

She'd seen St Jude's before. From a distance. And envied them each time, even if the building did send chills down her spine every time she looked at it.

At least it had a roof.

Young boys of all ages crouched and huddled in small groups in the mud-covered courtyard, yet it was eerily silent. Their home-made toys of sticks and strings dangled in frozen hands as all the children stopped and stared at the two visitors.

Then scattered.

It sent an unsettling shudder through Reed's heart. Like she wasn't welcome.

Probably wasn't.

Still, she dared herself to keep moving forward, and then paused as she let Devitt up the front step first to knock on the heavy door knocker.

The thud of metal on wood rattled through the silent grounds, but it brought no answer for some time.

Until, finally, a heavy deadbolt screeched in its latch from within, and the door groaned open.

A woman stood there, still and uninviting. To where Reed stood on the muddy ground behind the step, she looked so tall and controlling. Too severe. An apron over a dark wool dress. Gloves on. Dark brown hair pinned in a no-nonsense bun and an expression carved from soapstone.

'Yes?' There was no warmth in her voice.

Reed gulped. Let her eyes glance over at Devitt's back, glad to let him do the talking.

'Detective Inspector Devitt,' he said as he stepped a little further into the mouth of the entryway. He tipped his hat. 'And this is Constable Reed.'

Reed's heart fluttered as he gestured towards her with that title, making her sound fancier than she was. The woman's eyes barely flushed over her, but that didn't matter.

'We're investigating the Beechworth case,' Devitt continued smoothly, voice a little politer than normal. 'We have reason to believe one of your former residents may be connected.'

The woman stared for a moment, her pale eyes flickering between them. Clearly assessing.

'Of course you are,' she said, and stepped aside to let them in. 'It was only a matter of time.'

Reed frowned as she stepped in, but straightened her face and back as she walked past the woman in the doorway, as if she were still a child and the woman would have some power over her.

Well ... some element of that was right.

Reed noticed the woman reset the deadbolt after the door shut behind them.

Locking us in, some childish part of Reed's brain panicked. Before she tried to reassure herself. Tell herself that of course members of the police station wouldn't be locked inside an old orphanage.

'I'm the matron of this establishment,' the woman said, turning and marching past them down the hallway. 'I know who you're here for.' Her voice was strong, but higher-pitched. Strained. 'You're not the first to come here asking questions about him, you know.'

She paused and shot a dry look back at them. Brushed down an already immaculate apron.

'But you might be the first to come about his *smiling ones*, am I right?'

Her face said it all. She knew. It irked Reed how she'd known. But the woman marched on again, through dark corridors that were almost the complete opposite to the Beechworth townhouse's stark yet clean walls.

'It was always just about trespassing before. Fights, petty theft. I wonder how he kept the rest hidden for so long.'

The matron fiddled with the keys hung on her belt as she guided them up narrow wooden stairs. Reed noticed how her hands shook. The soft rattling of keys. Was it the cold, or ...?

'As soon as I saw the papers, I knew someone would eventually come looking.'

A flame of indignation fired through Reed's veins. 'Why didn't you come to us yourself if you knew something?' she asked, trying to hold back the bite but failing to remain polite and in control as she'd hoped. Like Devitt had been.

The matron turned to her, and for a moment, the haunted, anxious look of prey – like some kind of terrified rabbit – paled the woman's face. But only for a moment. Soon, long-practised professionalism had replaced it, and she glared down the steps at Reed.

'Time, mostly,' she snapped. 'Understaffed as we are, how often do you imagine I'm able to leave this place for a joyful jaunt through Town?'

And then she turned on her heels, skirts wrapping around her legs, and continued her march up the steps, leaving Reed feeling utterly chastised.

Just like a child.

They were led up another level of dingy stairs.

'Now,' the matron said, her voice quieter again. Clouded with worry. 'We must be quick. It'll be nightfall soon. And we *never* talk about *him* after dark.'

There was a door at the end of a dark corridor, and Reed strained to look past Devitt and Matron to see feathers and dead flowers and a scattering of coins left on the floor in front of it. She wrinkled her nose. Something didn't sit right with her.

But Matron simply tutted.

'He's not lived here for years,' she said. 'But the kids still leave him offerings.'

Reed noticed the woman made an effort not to touch them, though, as she leant forwards to unlock the door.

Devitt turned back to meet Reed's gaze as they waited, and the young woman was surprised to notice a hint of uncertainty in the detective's eyes.

Reed looked past him again. Noticed chalk stars all over the door. Some with smiles inside. Others that same constellation she'd always seen.

A crescent moon, with two stars to the right. The second circled.

The matron crossed herself as she continued fumbling with the keys. They clattered as her hands shook – more noticeable now – and when she finally found the right key, it scraped in the door hole.

'The room's been locked ever since he left,' she said, turning halfway back but not enough to look at them. 'The other kids refused to come in here, so we locked it. Some say they still hear music.' She sniffed and then gave them a severe look back as she swung open the door and stepped back to make room for them to enter. 'I tell them it's rats.'

Devitt stepped in first, but something made Reed pause at the threshold. She stared, tried to be brave. To move legs that suddenly felt like weighted ice, as if she'd jumped in the Thames in winter.

A desperation to prove herself pushed Reed forwards, and she followed Devitt inside.

The room was a mess of chalk scrawls, feathers, and bones. She squinted in the dim light, catching scratches in the wooden floor that Reed thought could only have been made with a knife. Patterns and circles she couldn't identify.

'You said he was obsessed with faerie circles and liked to kill birds?'

Reed gave Devitt a mute nod. She was certain her face looked as disturbed as his did.

'That's right,' Matron said. 'Always bringing back them dead birds. Plucking them. Leaving them to rot. Gathering the bones. Awful smell.'

The woman waited outside the room, but peered in with a grimace. 'And he'd leave the feathers in other children's beds. Nasty habit. Said it "marked them for flight". We never understood what he meant by that.'

Reed's body chilled. She shoved her hands into her coat pockets and shrugged her shoulders deeper into the collar, always wishing it could help hide her. Something about this nagged at her. Hung on the edge of memories she didn't want to remember.

She pulled herself to the present. Saw Devitt staring at her with those same eyes he always had when he was reading someone. Knew he'd ask her later.

Fortunately, Matron drew their attention. 'As you can see,' she said, still hiding in the doorway, 'he was a disturbed child. If you've come to dredge up stories, I suggest you speak to the children. They're the ones who keep his memory alive.'

Reed found it interesting that now the matron had started talking, she seemed unable to stop. Like all this had been trapped and bubbling inside her this whole time, begging for someone to listen to her.

Well, Reed understood *that*.

'You speak as if he's dead,' Devitt said, giving another stroll around the room. Reed watched how he scanned everything. How he crouched and inspected the faerie circles made of bird bones. Frowned at dark stains seeping into the wooden floorboards.

Matron let out a snort, but covered it with a whispered mutter of a prayer. 'Perhaps that would have been better.'

Devitt sighed, and Reed hoped he'd get what he needed over with as soon as possible so they could leave. The room stunk. There was a strange stillness and blocked energy in the room, though the window was broken and the wind whispered in so it should have been icy and fresh inside.

Finally, 'We've seen enough,' Devitt said. But Reed caught how choked his voice sounded.

Perhaps he wanted to leave just as much as she and the matron clearly did.

Reed hurried gratefully over the threshold, giving the room one last glance to make sure she hadn't been dreaming. Even with the broken window, the room seemed never to breathe. As if it had been frozen in time since the day the boy had left.

She shuddered. The last thing she saw before turning away was the skeleton of a bird lying in a circle of chalk stars.

And a smile etched into a star.

Devitt

Devitt had barely crossed the threshold before the matron had slammed the door behind him. Keys shook in the lock, sealing it off from the real world once more.

Matron strode away immediately, heels clacking on the wooden boards harder than before as if she were grounding herself through sound and feigned control.

'I wasn't matron then,' she called back to them as they rushed to follow. Of course, Devitt noticed how her voice shook. 'Just the assistant. Until the last matron died of sudden circumstances one night.'

She paused at the top of the steps and glanced back at them.

'When *he* was here.'

And then she stomped down the stairs, pausing a moment to tut over a scrape in a floorboard. Though, as far as Devitt could see, all the floorboards were entirely scraped and worn.

'No one thought anything of it at the time. Natural, they thought. Died in her sleep. But when I moved into her room to take over her duty, I found a chalk drawing of skulls and crossbones above her bed.'

She let out a choked laugh.

'Silly of me, isn't it? To worry over children's drawings.'

Devitt noticed she moved faster, almost fleeing.

'Children lie,' she continued. 'They lie and steal and tell stories about fae and pirates.'

Devitt glanced into the shared rooms as they passed. Neat, sterile rows of beds.

'When did he move into his own room?' he asked.

Matron stepped onto the final landing. Frowned as she thought about it for a moment.

'When the younger children said they couldn't sleep for the haunting stories and lullabies. Or hearing the ripping of feathers torn from the bodies of birds.'

Devitt winced.

'Can you blame us, Detective?' Matron asked, her voice hardening again. 'For any of this? No one would take him off us. This is the final place children like him go, after all. Until they run away, end up dead, or tossed in prison.'

The matron's heels echoed on the stone floors and walls around them as she quick marched them back to the front door, clearly hurrying them away.

Night was coming.

The woman unbolted the door. Heaved it open.

'All I can say is I'm glad we don't have to hear those creepy songs or lullabies or pan pipes of his any more,' she said. Sniffed and picked up a giant bell from the floor by the door. 'Not that they'll ever leave my head until the day I can join the Lord above and he can finally free me of this madness.' She clenched her jaw. 'But until then ...'

A harsh wind blew and sent a chill through them all. Devitt shivered and pulled his coat closer. He turned back to look at

Reed, who'd already nearly fully disappeared into her oversized trench coat.

'And now it's dark,' the matron snapped. 'I told you, we don't speak of him after dark.' She gave him a firm nod. Even Reed, he noticed. 'Good day, Detective, Constable.' Then she stepped out onto the cracked stone slab step outside, ringing the bell that called all the children back inside for the evening.

'Our cue to leave,' Devitt muttered to the silent Reed hiding in her coat beside him.

The bell's chime followed them down the street, thin and reedy through the fog, and Devitt couldn't shake the feeling that somewhere in London, the haunting pan pipe lullaby had already begun again.

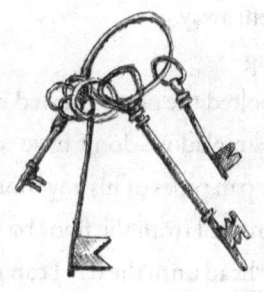

6

A Party for the Dead

Devitt

Devitt didn't go home that night. How could he, with so few clues and Beechworth and the mayor breathing down his neck? The trip to St Jude's had been eye-opening – and utterly chilling – but going to the old bedroom and listening to stories about an orphaned boy who liked telling creepy tales and plucking birds for their bones didn't bring him any closer to Pan.

He spent the night hunched over his desk, flipping through the files he and Reed had set aside on children with similar deaths. How did Matron's stories tie in? What connection did they have to Beechworth and his rise in politics? And if Pan was no longer at St Jude's but still roaming London, how could they find him?

Cheek pressed into his fist, Devitt's eyes blurred across the pages. Names and dates merged into indistinct smudges. But he still forced himself upright, irritated at his own persistence.

No luck.

The spluttering candlelight barely lit the letters for him to focus on them anyway, so he ended up sleeping on the floor behind his desk, just enough to keep going, though his bones protested.

By the time Reed stormed in the next morning – straight up to his office, this time, he noticed – Devitt's head was no clearer, and nor was the case.

Her grey eyes swept over his rugged appearance, lips pursed. 'You slept here?'

Devitt opened his mouth to deny it but caught himself. She'd slept on streets as a child; of course she knew the signs.

'Sometimes it happens,' he admitted. 'Especially when a high-profile person is demanding you find the murderer of his children immediately.'

Reed frowned. 'It's not that easy.'

Devitt threw out his hands. 'Now try telling them that.' And then he ran his hands through his dusty hair to try to bring some semblance of neatness to it. 'Did you notice yesterday Matron never gave us time to speak to the other children?'

Reed gave a small nod and then looked over at the murky window. 'But you can ask them any time. The kids of St Jude's always get out.'

'But how'd we know it's them?' Devitt racked through his brain. All the children in that lifeless yard had been wearing normal clothes. Not some kind of uniform. No way to recognise them.

'You just know,' Reed said, shrugging.

He sighed. That would require her help later. But for now, the gala had priority. Beechworth's instructions came first: protect him and his wife tonight, even without knowing how to identify Pan.

Devitt groaned and slouched back in his chair. 'Any chance you know what Pan looks like?'

The young woman scoffed lightly. Turned and leant back on his desk and folded her arms. 'No,' she said. 'I *knew* there was something we didn't ask Matron. It was all too focused on faerie stories.'

'As if he's not really human,' Devitt added.

She nodded.

'I want you to come with me to the gala tonight,' Devitt said, leaning forwards again and picking up his pencil. 'You're well in the know and sharp. Will keep a good eye out.'

Reed looked down at her shoes. Not the reaction Devitt was expecting, certainly. 'I heard you call me *Constable* to Matron,' she said quietly.

'Makes sense,' he said. 'Made her listen to you too. And you're good enough for it.'

Her eyes flickered up for a moment, but she didn't say anything. Devitt didn't mind. Instead, his head spiralled at whether he should keep pulling her into this. Whether it was too dark or dangerous to bring such a young woman into. But they were interrupted by a knock at the door before he could even ask how she felt at being so involved in such a case.

A street urchin – running as a messenger.

The boy thrust something into Devitt's hand before quickly tipping his hat and dashing off again, leaving Devitt staring at the empty doorway.

Reed coughed, and they both looked down at the item in Devitt's hands.

A feather – sleek, black, like a crow's, but with a white, powdery tip.

Devitt peered closer, holding it up in the weak grey ray of daylight slanting in through his window. No, the feather's tip wasn't naturally white. There was white powder on his fingers from where he'd held it.

Chalk.

Reed

Reed had never imagined anything like the gala: glittering chandeliers, candles along sandstone walls, string instruments wailing over the murmur of high-up guests laughing and chattering in elaborate attire. Women in flowing dresses and jewels, men in tailcoats and starched collars, all clinging to flutes of pale gold bubbles.

Not to mention an incredibly suffocating blend of overly strong perfume clashing with the curling smoke trails of countless cigars.

She hugged the collars of her oversized coat and edged along the walls. The wife was missing, reportedly haunted by bad dreams. But Beechworth was there: charming, composed, laughing, the picture of social ease. Not at all the image of a man who had just lost three children.

'Not that he looked like this when I met him at the mayor's office yesterday,' Devitt had grumbled when Reed asked him about it.

She sniffed and continued. Devitt had told her to stroll the edge. Keep a watch for anything unusual.

But it was all unusual for her here.

A small boy in formal clothes and holding hands with his mother caught her attention. She'd not expected to see a child here.

Guessed it was normal for the higher-ups, so continued her plod of the hall.

Fancy little gems of finger food were passed around on platters by well-dressed waiters. Foods nothing like Reed had seen before.

She let her eyes flicker to them now and then – a curiosity she knew she'd never sedate – as her brain grumbled about something else entirely. About what Pan even wanted with Beechworth, anyway.

A grown man.

When all his life he'd haunted children.

Revenge at the system? she wondered. For being thrown into St Jude's? Not cared about? For so many people in charge letting the problem of children on the streets just wash over them?

That she could understand. It's why she'd done anything she could to get work at the station. Hung about and been useful until they'd forgotten she wasn't even supposed to be there. But that reasoning all seemed too noble for Pan, who seemed to have fun in his twisted imaginings.

He'd broken birds apart and kept them as decorations in his bedroom, after all.

She dodged a waiter.

Maybe Pan was actually older than everyone thought, and Beechworth had been a child at the same time. Jealousy or fighting one another.

But that seemed far too stretched. Pan was active when she was a street kid, and not having been for long, it seemed.

So he was only a few years older than her. At most.

Reed wrinkled her nose as she scanned the room for the unusual. Too much glitz. Too many people. How on earth were they supposed to find someone targeting Beechworth amongst this? Anyone could be hiding anywhere.

She blinked and forced herself to focus. Noticed the small boy from earlier walking off on his own through one of the doors that led to outside.

Looked back at the boy's mother, deep in conversation with a round man the other side of the hall.

Odd.

Surely you wouldn't let such a small child just wander off on his own?

Reed jogged to catch up with him and crouched down in front of him, trying on her best smile.

'Did you lose your mum?' she asked.

He looked startled to see her, but it softened immediately to a small smile. Shook his head. 'I saw a boy with leaves in his hair. He wanted to show me a feather.'

Reed's breath stuttered, and her hands tightened against his shoulders.

'Your mother is so worried,' she said, trying to smile reassuringly while shooting quick glances around them to see if she could spot a child-luring creep hiding around them. 'She's looking everywhere for you inside. Let's go back together and see her.'

The boy gave her a look of such wide-eyed innocence that only such a tiny child could muster, and it churned at Reed's stomach. She took his hand and guided him back inside, not letting go until it was instead clutched into the mother's.

'Keep a tight hand. Don't let go,' she warned.

The mother's face paled instantly.

And rightly so. After all, Reed knew now how many children might have been targeted by Pan. And even though she still couldn't figure out what Pan wanted with Beechworth, she could at least stop *this* child from being in any trouble too.

But what the boy had said ... a boy with leaves in his hair. A feather.

So Pan *had* come? As Devitt predicted.

Reed was drawn back to that door the boy had walked through. If Pan had been outside, trying to show him something ... If a feather had been 'the mark of flight' as Matron had said, then would that boy have been next?

Did that mean Pan was out here, and she'd just ruined his plan?

He'd be annoyed. Perhaps had already moved. But she had to try to search for him anyway.

She peered around the doorway as subtly as she could before stepping through it. Shivered a little at leaving the overly candle-heated hall for the freezing night air. Scanned the area for a boy with leaves stuck in his hair.

It took a while, in the dark, with so many trees filling the garden. But finally, she saw someone perched on a thick tree branch, looking through a grand window into the tumbling hall of higher-ups.

And, yes, he seemed just a few years older than herself. And the leaves the small child had told her about had been woven into some kind of crown.

Fancying himself a faerie king, Reed sneered to herself.

The leaf boy hadn't noticed her yet, so she snuck out further, curious about what he was watching through the large window.

Devitt.

He was standing in front of the window at the edge of the gala, back to the garden, watching whatever was going on inside.

No. He was inspecting something in his hand.

Reed squinted. Paper. Instructions from the station? No. A photograph of a family by the looks of it. How did he even have a photograph? Devitt didn't even seem that well off.

Devitt folded the photograph and placed it inside his overcoat pocket. Returned his gaze to the room. Strode around the edge again, hands behind his back, leaving the view of the window.

Inside, a violin warbled a loud and high-pitched note that made Reed jolt to attention even outside. And then her heart kicked back up, eyes returning to the trees to find Pan now staring at her.

He grinned, pressed a finger to his lips.

A cold wind cut between them, rustling through the trees and whipping her hair across her face.

When she looked again, he was gone.

7

The Window at Home

Reed

Reed stomped through the busy streets the next morning, dodging pickpockets without even looking. She stepped over a tumbling mess of fruit as someone knocked over a market stall basket. Ignored it. She knew that trick. Stopping to help them pick it up would get her robbed.

The bustle was deafening as usual – not that she wasn't used to it – but today, stuck in her own thoughts, Reed could barely focus on anything. Newspaper boys hawked for attention at nearly every crossing, and there was a young busker trying to play an old fiddle in the corner near the butcher.

A street kid, by the looks of him.

Girls could never busk. It had been something that had irked at Reed this whole time – the lack of fair ways to beg for coin. Girls would get offers of other things tossed at them instead of coins, or money held back with biting bribes.

So that's where the market tricks came in.

But amongst all this usual background noise, the abnormal haunted her. The grin that Pan had shot her when he'd noticed her watching him. Even in this chaotic crowd, the memory made her uneasy.

His eyes like a corpse. Hollow. Depthless. Ageless. With the look that he had no fear whatsoever that she had a chance to catch him.

Reed shrugged deeper into her overcoat collar. Stepped into the police station and stomped the dirt off her boots near the door before sidling her way through to her little nook off to the back edge. Hid amongst all the cabinets.

She sighed. Tried to shake it all off. But when it wasn't working, and her heart just wouldn't ease, she glared up at the ceiling.

Devitt would be here already, surely?

Unable to get the thoughts of Pan out of her head, she turned her mind to practicalities instead. Turned on the spot and jogged up the narrow, creaking steps to find the spiritless detective.

She peered around the door.

As expected, he was here. And matching what she'd guessed from yesterday, it seemed he'd been here all night again. Now, he was slumped half asleep over a desk buried in paper. Behind it, a blanket and quilt gave away what he clearly hoped no one would notice.

But that was Reed's whole identity. Even now. A makeshift bed pushed together with a bunch of other girls in a small single room.

At least they were inside now.

So, of course she'd notice the signs that Devitt was sleeping rough, too.

'Devitt?' she tested.

The man looked up, eyes glassy with fatigue.

'You good?' she asked.

He took a sharp inhale and looked up at her. Leant back in his chair. Sighed. 'Good?' He rubbed a prickly jaw with his hand. 'Not exactly the way I'd describe this current predicament.'

Reed raised a brow. Nudged a little more. 'The case, or ...'

She let her gaze wander to the quilts behind him to do the talking. The detective startled. Shifted. Turned in his seat and kicked it all more behind his desk.

'Beechworth's not exactly the sort to allow breaks,' he muttered.

Reed merely nodded. He'd mentioned something about that the morning before.

'Hey,' she started. 'You need to watch out. Pan's watching you.'

'Of course he is,' Devitt said, adjusting papers on his desk. 'He's playing games with us. Crims do that all the time. Think they're smart. Want to see our reactions.'

'No, he was watching you look at that photograph you have in your pocket.'

That hit him. She saw it in his eyes and how he straightened. But then he brushed it off almost instantly. 'He'll be watching all of us. You included. To see who's a threat. How much time he has. Where we are in the case.'

Then his eyes met hers with raised brows that wrinkled his forehead.

'But, I think it's *you* who needs to be more concerned. You're still more child than adult, if I'm not mistaken, now, eh?'

Reed froze. Heat flooded her whole body in a flash.

'I—I don't know what you're talking about,' she stammered. 'I'm of age.'

'Yes, but of *what* age?' Devtit asked, his voice low. 'I'm starting to think more and more you're *not* nineteen like you told us?'

She stared. Didn't know how to answer.

'You said yourself you were on the streets for a few years, just a while back.'

Reed kicked herself. This is why she never talked about her past. But this case had thrown her right back there. Made her remember things.

'Time blurs on the streets,' she said, waving it off. 'And when you're finally off them. I didn't mean it *exactly*. A few years. A while back. You know ...'

Devitt rose, and Reed couldn't help but step back.

No. She was going to be found out. Found out and fired. But she needed this job. It paid poorly, but it *paid*. She was already hanging on by splinters. Just enough wages to keep her shared roof. Not be thrown back to the streets.

And this job would help her achieve her goal.

Devitt stepped slowly around his desk, almost like he was wary not to startle a stray cat.

'How old are you, Reed?'

She froze.

'Less than nineteen?' he pushed. Paused beside his desk, and she was grateful for the distance.

'Less than nineteen.'

'Less than seventeen?'

She clamped her jaw shut.

Dared to nod and then clenched her fists and waited for the outburst. To be fired.

But Devitt didn't yell, shout, or kick her out. Instead, he sighed. Stepped back. Ran a hand through his greying hair and stared at her with those pale green eyes with a look she had recently learnt to hate from him.

Because it was far more sympathetic than she was used to. Or liked. It made things unpredictable.

'I figured,' he said finally, turning away and letting his gaze and hand drop to fiddle with reports on the desk. 'Not all along,' he added quickly. 'You're safe. Just—'

He tilted his head. Gestured to the papers. 'Just recently. Things you said.'

She clamped her lips shut.

Devitt sat heavily into his chair and took a swig of whatever was in the clay mug on his desk. Looked over his desk with a gaze that suggested he had no idea where to start.

Reed looked at it too, if only because she didn't know what else to do now.

Her eyes caught the sleek black crow feather half hidden amongst the papers, right next to a half written letter.

'You know,' Devitt said, drawing her attention again. 'When that came in yesterday, I worried he might come for you.'

He was looking at the feather too.

'To scare you. Get you off the case. Leave us with fewer people in the know. You're the one who joined the dots, after all. Maybe it takes a child's eyes.'

He paused. Looked up at her.

'Sorry, not child. Just … closer.' He tilted his head in thought. 'Stuck in the middle, perhaps. Like him.'

Reed wanted to stand her ground. Ask whether her secret was safe and whether she could stay in this job, but the half written letter caught her eye again.

Martha,
Tell the kids I—

So he hadn't got any further since he'd started writing it that day she'd last seen it. Still had the half-hearted star drawing in the corner.

'I still don't think he's here for me,' she breathed.

She was just a child. How could she persuade him to go home and check on his family when he was clearly stressed about the case?

But before either of them could say anything further, the man who supposedly liaised with the media for them – Chattoway, was it? – popped his head around Devitt's door.

Called him away to the supervisor's office for a debrief of the Beechworth party the night before.

Devitt nodded warily, and Chattoway disappeared after a slimy remark that left Devitt curling his lip.

'Well,' Devitt grunted as he rose. 'Best go. We'll keep on at the case later. After I've no doubt been strung up by the supervisor for this case taking too long.'

He grimaced as he left, leaving Reed wondering at the bad relationship between the two men.

Unsure of what else to do left standing in his office like this, her eyes roamed the room. All the reports they'd reviewed over the last couple of days were strewn carelessly across his desk. And though Reed desperately wanted to regather them into some semblance of order – maybe check the information again to see whether there was anything she had missed – it was still the letter her eyes kept returning to.

And the feather next to it.

She wished she could shake Devitt by the collar and make him see that it was *him* being haunted next.

But unable to do that, she grabbed the letter. Folded it neatly and shoved it in her pocket.

Shut Devitt's door on her way out.

Reed turned a final corner until her eyes met the street sign she was looking for, pointing to a small street of simple townhouses pushed right up against the path. No fancy gates and gardens here. And, surprisingly, Devitt's house was a small stone thing, squashed between many others that all looked the same.

Nothing like she thought a detective inspector would live in. She thought he'd have something grander.

But then she thought back to Devitt's near constant dishevelled appearance. So it *wasn't* just from being tired and overworked. He was hanging on just as much as most people in London.

Reed let out a small breath. Stepped forwards and knocked on the front door.

A small woman opened it.

'Martha Devitt?' Reed tested when the woman searched her with suspicious eyes.

But then, of course she did. Reed knew she looked dodgy. A tiny young girl in an oversized police coat. Looked more like she'd stolen it than wore it officially.

She tapped her old flat cap and clicked her heels like all the others did. Smart. Sharp, even, she hoped. Trying to belong.

'Constable Reed, ma'am,' she said, hoping it was okay to use the fake title Devitt had given her just one last time. 'Detective Inspector Devitt sent me to pass on a message.'

Martha's shoulders relaxed a little. 'Um, yes, right. Come in, I suppose.'

She shuffled out of the way, and as the door opened more, Reed noticed a toddler clinging to Martha's hip, protectively out of sight behind the door. The boy's large green eyes stared at her, and Reed pulled a little face as she entered.

The boy's eyes widened a little before Martha turned and led her down the hallway.

'Would you like a cup of tea?'

Martha's voice echoed down the narrow hallway as Reed stayed back to push the door shut behind them. She paused before she followed, guilt gnawing at her. She'd already stolen Devitt's letter and used a fake title. Being welcomed in with tea seemed too much.

'You look cold,' Martha added, pausing in the doorway at the end of the hall.

'It *is* cold out,' Reed said, rubbing her hands together for heat, hoping that was permission enough. She padded over the worn wood floor after Martha.

But she'd never been to someone's house for tea before. What was she meant to do?

Martha bustled about the kitchen, handling everything despite the toddler on her hip. Reed felt awkward, hugging the side of the room and trying to figure out her place before finally giving up after watching Martha navigate open flame with one hand to light the burner.

'Here,' Reed lunged forward. 'Let me. You sit.'

Martha looked uncertain for a moment, before giving a small smile and placing the wick in Reed's outstretched hand as she turned to take a nearby chair. She adjusted the toddler to sit on her lap, and the boy leant back happily.

'It's a bit strange to have a guest making me tea in my own house!' Martha said with a light chuckle, but when Reed glanced back, the young mother looked relieved.

'Must be tricky with the kids,' was all Reed said, her hands shaking a little with the match.

'Sometimes,' Martha said, her voice trailing off. 'Especially the burner.' Reed looked back as Martha paused. Watched her looking down and fondly stroking the boy's head.

Then Reed remembered the paper in her pocket. Took the opportunity while waiting for the water in the pan to boil on the flame and passed the letter to Martha.

'The detective asked me to give you this,' she gushed. 'Sorry, he said it was unfinished. He was called away as he started writing it. But wanted you to know he hated having to stay away. Thought about you all.'

Devitt may not speak about his family, but he was easy to read.

Martha's eyes widened in surprise as she took the letter. Read the few words on the paper. And then her face closed up, and she nodded.

Then, 'He's not pushing you too hard, is he?'

Reed blinked. Knitted her brows together as her brain worked too slowly over it. Turned from where she watched the pan. Devitt's wife was asking about her?

But Martha's face was clear. Genuine.

Reed turned back to the burner. It was easier to talk this way. Without looking. No expression read. No emotions seen. She watched the flickering orange glow instead.

'You're so pale,' Martha added. 'Are you sleeping all right? Do you have time to eat? I hope my husband's not too strict on you. You're so young.'

Reed's heart pulsed, and her throat tightened. She wasn't used to so much concern.

'Your husband is a good detective,' Reed said, trying to keep her voice steady. 'It's *his* boss we need to be careful of. And the politician. Always chasing the detective. Never giving him time. They want this case solved as soon as possible.'

Martha sighed, and Reed dared to look around to see what kind of face she was making.

Then running steps echoed through the wooden floorboards of the house and down the steps, and a girl crashed into the kitchen, her pale, curling hair tumbling about a smiling face. Light, happy eyes. 'Mummy!'

Martha's face instantly lit up, and Reed poured the tea awkwardly as the girl joined her mother at the table, crashing some pencils and paper onto it as she sat down. Martha guided Reed to some biscuits as an extra treat.

'This is Alice,' Martha said as Reed sat to join them at the table. 'Alice, this is Reed. She works for Daddy. Daddy says sorry he's working too much!'

Reed stared as she hugged the clay mug in her hands. Gave a soft, hesitant nod when Martha gestured for her to take a biscuit.

'Sorry,' Martha said between sips of her own tea. 'They're a little dry.'

But biscuits were a luxury to Reed, half-stale as they were. And dipped into the tea, the warmth soaking into the biscuit before it melted in her mouth? There was no way she could complain.

Martha seemed half dreamy as she watched her kids. The toddler had been given his own pencil and was scribbling recklessly on an old piece of paper, while Alice focused on what Reed could make out a little to be some kind of house.

And through sips of hot tea, Martha softly gave sympathetic comments about not blaming her husband for feeling pressure to stay in such a high-profile case. How she'd heard about it from the street newspaper boys and knew a little. The poor children. The poor mother. And with Reed unsure of how much Martha knew, she kept quiet, just nibbling her biscuit and offering appreciative nods and hums of polite listening.

Then a comfortable silence fell, and both women stared at the children drawing. Martha began humming a tune to herself, with Alice joining in as she drew.

It sent a chill down Reed's spine.

'Where's that song from?' she asked, nervously.

Martha looked up at her absent-mindedly. 'Hm? Oh.' And then she frowned. 'Actually, I'm not sure. You've been humming it recently, haven't you, darling?'

She ran her fingers through her daughter's yellow hair fondly, and the girl looked up with a grin.

'It's a song for an adventure!'

Reed's heart stuttered. The trio on the other side of the small wooden table seemed happy enough, lost in their cosy drawings. Didn't even notice her discomfort. But everything in Reed's skin crawled, and with a sudden urge to move, she gulped the last of her tea. Thanked Martha. Jumped up and washed the cup. And then dismissed herself saying Devitt would need her back for help.

She was already marching down the hallway as Martha called after her to take care of herself.

Reed scrunched her eyes up as she shut the front door carefully behind her, taking a great breath of fresh air to calm herself. Convincing herself it was another song. A coincidence.

There are no coincidences in policing, she told herself. Repeating what someone had told her on her first day as assistant. Told her to drill it into her head.

She took another breath. Was about to walk back to the station when on the pavement just ahead of her feet, she noticed a chalk star on one of the stone slabs in front of Devitt's house.

How had she not noticed that earlier? Had she been so focused on looking at the door numbers that she'd missed it?

With her heart in her throat, she turned on the spot. Looked at the house from the perspective of the star, wondering which window had best view of it.

Top right window.

And if she stood on her tiptoes, she could just about see a feather resting lightly on the windowsill.

8

The Lost Smile

Reed

She had to tell Devitt. That much, she knew. But how? That would involve admitting she'd stolen his letter and gone to his house without his knowing?

Of course he would be uncomfortable about it. She'd be in so much trouble.

But despite the anxiety gnawing like a rat through her stomach, she ran up the narrow wooden steps to his office as soon as she darted into the station.

Not there.

This sent another rat to her stomach. And it wasn't made any better by asking others where he might be. Other constables half ignored her – like always, until they wanted some paperwork done or a horse called for – and one decided to get some long-needed grumblings off his chest.

Told her Devitt was on Beechworth duty and not to be interrupted by 'someone lowly of the likes of her' in such an important case, and that though she might have helped the detective with a few things on the case, to not get grand ideas about her own importance.

Reed fumed. Stormed off and flumped into her wonky seat in the corner of the filing cabinets.

She already knew who she was. That it was impossible being a female in Scotland Yard, and that even being accepted as an assistant in the station was miracle enough.

But still ...

She rested her head on her desk, ignoring the smell of old varnish and bug-eaten wood, wondering what to do next.

That day, Reed stayed late at the station, pretending to catch up on paperwork, just to try to grab Devitt when he came back to inevitably work late and bunk there.

But he still didn't come back. No matter how long the shadows stretched and how the oil lamps were lit to ward off the growing dark – not that the light reached her little corner.

She glanced over at the collection of constables shifting around in the main room to her left. Wasting time, for the most of it. And though she knew they wouldn't tell her if she went to ask about Devitt, she could just about catch mumblings of them chatting to one another instead. That Devitt was having to stay on watch at the Beechworth place to see if the killer came back.

You've got the wrong house! she screamed to them all in her head.

And then it clicked, and she straightened a little in her chair. It had never been about the politician. It was always the children.

Even back on the streets, only children.

Pan lured other children around him into his sick game. Remembered what Alice had said about the song.

A song for an adventure.

So Pan was tricking them with talk about adventures. Convincing them into some kind of better life, whatever it was. And as desperate as she was to find out what he was saying to them, now, she had to prioritise helping the children. The next feather had already been played, and Devitt's daughter was marked for flight.

She shot up.

It was so obvious now. Kids marked for flight. Bedroom windows. Children on the ground. No traces of breaking and entering or of violence.

Smiles on their faces.

Flight.

They'd jumped on their own.

—well, been persuaded.

But they'd jumped *willingly*. Believed they were going to fly.

Reed gasped and grabbed her coat from where she'd dumped it to the side. Pulled it on as she dashed out, boots loud on rain-slick cobblestones. She clenched her jaw together, begging to get there in time.

Alice was marked for flight. There was no waiting for Devitt now.

Devitt

It was cold and dark, and this was utterly pointless. Devitt was pacing outside just to keep warm, hiding his lower face in his scarf from the cool wind.

His eyes roamed the silence of towering, clean townhouses down Arlington Street. Nothing stirred. The stretching shadows from the flickering flames of the street lamps was the creepiest thing here, and that was nothing to be concerned about.

Devitt sighed and turned. Paced again, closer to number 12. Caught the gaze of a constable who'd come here with him.

The man shook his head.

Still nothing.

Devitt curled his lips and watched the neat layers of rooftops. If Pan could climb, he *might* be leaping around up there like a shadow, and then jumping through windows – risky as it was. But if someone had such a mission that drove them to killing, nothing seemed impossible.

And still, Devitt couldn't figure out why Beechworth would be the target. The man had been safe at the political gathering, and his wife had been safe when she stayed at home. Devitt was *certain* Pan wasn't after Beechworth, but had no way to prove it yet.

He glared at the ornate iron gate that led into Beechworth's front garden. Standing here felt utterly wrong, but there was still no proof to convince his superintendent to drop the watch on Beechworth.

And where had Reed buggered off to earlier? Devitt was certain she'd have discovered something new, but what with being sent here on watch before she'd returned, he'd not been able to ask her what she'd learnt.

He shoved his hands in his pockets for warmth.

'If Pan wanted Beechworth dead, he'd be dead,' he grumbled into his scarf.

The rooftops around Beechworth's house were clear. No feathers, no ghostly boys leaping over chimneys, and no lilting lullabies on pan pipes. This area was dead.

A chill overcame him, so Devitt stomped his feet and paced again. Thought back to the black feather the street kid had delivered to his office. It was a warning – no doubt about that. Telling them to back off, most likely. But who was it aimed at?

So far, Pan seemed only to go after children. All those reports of similar deaths had been children, with no luck in finding similar deaths in adults when he'd asked Reed to search the reports for more. But there was only one person close to the age of a child at Scotland Yard.

His heart flared. Reed?

If Pan was warning them off the case, he could be targeting Reed next.

Everything in his body tried to tear him away from that spot and find her. But with no clue where she lived, and strict instructions to stay here personally to watch Beechworth's house for the night, Devitt took all his willpower to stay put.

But what then of Reed?

He could whistle for one of the other constables. Send one as a runner. See if they could find her. But that would be breaking orders, and he had no evidence to tell the superintendent why he'd disobeyed and *risk* a high parliament member on a whim.

Devitt ground his teeth. Stayed put for now and hoped he had it wrong. Hoped Reed could handle herself if she was in the know about the case.

He sniffed. At least it wasn't raining, though that didn't stop the damp seeping into his bones.

It would be a long night.

Reed

Reed's boots slammed on stone pathways, and her breath came urgent and ragged.

How long did Pan leave it? Did it take long to persuade them? Get stories in their heads about that other world and then place the feather that signalled to them it was time?

Street lamps flickered in the puddles at her feet. She missed jumping over one. Puddle-spray sent ice shots up her leg.

Already, drunks dotted the streets, shuffling on the roads and slumping in alleyways and against buildings. Laughter from a distant bar and a muffled piano from a pub somewhere set unease in Reed's heart, and though she was used to being out at night, she could never stop the anxiety that gnawed at her around drunks.

But tonight she had a reason to push on. A desperation that drove her past all the drunks and pubs, despite the voice inside her that wanted to run and hide in her shared room.

She turned off the main streets down the little cul de sac where Devitt's home rested squashed in a row of townhouses. Suddenly, the streets were nearly silent.

Well, except for a tune. A soft, lilting lullaby played on pipes.

Reed froze, her stomach lurching. Listened closer.

It was the same lullaby the constable had badly hummed right at the start of this case. The same lullaby Martha had been humming only that afternoon. The lullaby Alice had echoed.

'No,' Reed breathed.

Bolted forwards again.

Reed never saw the three Beechworth children. But the stories she'd heard and the sketches she'd seen in the reports had etched at her enough that she couldn't stop picturing their glassy eyes and frozen smiles.

She wasn't ready to see that with Devitt's daughter.

Refused to.

She grit her teeth as she slipped over a cobblestone. Her ankle hurt, but what did that matter now? Especially when she couldn't get that bitter grumble out of her head: if only Devitt had listened to her earlier.

Devitt's house was just ahead, so Reed looked up, craning her neck and begging not to see the worst.

The feather was no longer on the windowsill. But Alice was.

Just climbing through from her bedroom onto the ledge, with a dreamy smile on her face and looking up at the sky as if searching for something, or someone.

Probably had no idea Reed was there just below her.

Reed's heart crumbled into crushed chalk powder and nearly clogged her throat. Blocked her voice from crying out.

Instead, she crashed through Devitt's front door – thank goodness Martha had left it unbolted for Devitt to come home – and threw herself up the stairs, yelling out Martha's name as she pushed through Alice's nursery door.

Alice was standing on the windowsill with her arms outstretched like a bird, hair and nightgown lifting in the light breeze.

Didn't look when Reed yelled out her name.

Reed's heart tugged her on. Somewhere behind her, Martha was calling out fearfully to whoever had burst into the house, but Reed couldn't wait. She darted forwards as Alice raised a leg to step forward.

Reed's arms wrapped around Alice's waist as the girl leant forward, and with a strained cry, she yanked Alice back, and both girls crashed to the floor.

Alice strained and flailed in her arms for a moment, but Reed refused to let go. Closed her eyes and held as tight as she could, saying Alice's name over and over again until the girl flopped against her. And then the child shuddered and cried, and Reed opened her eyes.

'He said I could fly,' Alice bawled.

Reed's blood flushed cold. And without knowing what else to do or say, she just lay there on the hard floor and stroked Alice's head.

'Alice?'

There was a shuffling in the door, and Reed looked up to see a pale Martha staring in horror.

'It was meant to be an adventure.' Alice's voice cracked and strained, and she curled up next to Reed and cried onto her shoulder.

Reed caught Martha's gaze. Sent a silent plea.

'It's okay,' Reed whispered as Martha understood and padded to join them. 'We've got you.'

9

Tell Me

Reed

Pan would still be there, watching. Reed knew it. She left the crying Alice in Martha's arms with a promise to be back, and then ran outside, stomping over that disturbing chalk star already half washed away by the rain.

Every inch of her was covered in an icy sweat, and her breath remained caught in her throat.

It had been too close.

Reed desperately scanned the dark street, and with the low fog slowly rolling in and the tall, tightly packed townhouses crowding in on her, the world seemed to trap her in, taunting.

Shadows loomed on the ground, but now she knew where to look. Up.

She tore her eyes from the frightful shadows and fog and searched the rooftops. A figure moved on the roof of a townhouse in the row opposite Devitt's house, and her heart jolted.

The figure dropped, landing deftly on the ground. Closer than she'd either expected or liked.

Pan.

He stepped beneath a flickering street lamp and leant against the pole, grinning. The flamelight flickered gently across his face, never quite settling, making it difficult to see him clearly. So Reed forced herself to look. To take in every detail she could – something to bring back to the station. Something useful.

Like at Beechworth's political gala, his hair was a tangle of loose locks – maybe mid brown but hard to tell in the dim orange glow – with that crown of leaves. A feather was tucked behind one ear, and it made Reed's stomach churn as she remembered all those bird bones back in his room at St Jude's. Almost like he was wearing bones for jewels.

He looked like some kind of spirit of the forest – if spirits had the pale eyes of a corpse.

'You found me!' His grin widened, too quick to be normal. 'Clever girl.'

Reed's skin crawled. And though she wanted desperately to run away, she ignored her pounding heart and stepped closer. For Alice.

For all of the children.

'Why are you doing this?' she growled, feeling a heat flush through so fast that she'd almost forget how cold the night was. That perhaps the cold sweat prickling at her skin would steam in an instant.

His smile held, and so did his annoyingly bright yet unsettlingly pale gaze.

'You took my next smile from me,' he said, ignoring her question entirely. 'And she so desperately wanted to join me and my Lost Boys on our adventure.'

He pushed himself off the lamp post. Took a few steps towards her until he was much too close for her liking and she realised just how much taller he was.

Not a child any more. Not quite.

And still Reed resisted the urge to step back. She'd be the one to stand her ground against him. If she wanted to get into Scotland Yard truly, she couldn't run away from a boy who was barely more than a child himself.

'Poor girl,' he said now, looking down at her. 'She so desperately wanted to meet the mermaids. And now Alice will have to live with the uncomfortable truth of growing old. Suffering. Such a dull life.'

Reed glared. 'Don't say her name,' she snapped. 'You're not allowed. And leave her alone.'

Pan let out a bark of a laugh, and the childish joy on his face made Reed want to slap it off him.

Someone had to, after all. Didn't they? After all this?

'You must know, after all, how unfair this life is,' he said, stretching up now and looking up at the sky as if he had made some grand discovery. He sighed dramatically. 'But up there in the stars ... look there ...'

He reached out his hand. Pointed a long, delicate finger.

Reed hated how persuasive he was. Hated how she looked.

'If we could reach the second star – yes, just there, just to the right – a better world awaits us there.'

And then he looked down at her again and smiled as if he'd been there for her all along. A brother, of some kind.

'You just need faith. And to trust me.'

Something inside Reed's body snapped. She sneered. Let a growl escape her lips. And was surprised that even Pan's face widened for a brief moment of letting go, and he stepped back just a little.

She was learning how to notice such tiny details, learning from the detectives, after all.

But Pan was too good at this game. Within a breath it was covered over, and he leant in again. Smiled like a corpse or some deranged thing. Worse than her uncle that time ...

'Oh, you're good. I knew you were.' Pan cocked his head and let his eyes roam over her.

Reed hid how uncomfortable it made her feel. Straightened her back. Stood like she saw Devitt stand whenever he actually acted like a proper detective rather than slouching over his desk like some tortured, overworked thing.

'So, you're my sister of the feathered lie ...'

He paused, and for a moment it looked as if his eyes had clouded over. As if he were still thinking, and Reed desperately wanted to know what came next.

What that even meant.

And then he grinned again. 'We're the same, you and me.'

She snapped. 'We're not the same.'

Pan leant in closer, until his nose almost touched hers. How she didn't yell and run away, Reed didn't know. She hated how desperate she was to prove herself here that she'd stand so close she could smell death and decay reeking off him.

'I'll tell you my name, if you tell me yours,' he said in a sing-song voice, locking her eyes into his corpse-grey stare.

Reed glared. Refused to blink. Refused to break first. She scowled and curled her hands into fists with her nails biting into her own palms just to remind her to stand there and be brave. Thought back to all the faerie circles and bird bones from his locked room at St Jude's.

The stories of him being obsessed with the fae.

'That's how you do it,' she breathed.

'Of course.'

He grinned. Stayed far too close, and Reed now knew it was a game. Loser was the one who moved first.

'Names are power, didn't you know?' Pan said. 'Heavy. Can't take flight without giving up the weight of your name.'

And then he tilted his head to the side and leant in closer, so much so that his face brushed past her cheek and her hair.

Now, this was far too close that Reed almost didn't mind being the loser if it meant she could move away. If only her legs would move. Instead, they were locked – almost by some spell.

'Go on,' he whispered in her ear, sending shivers zapping through her blood. 'Tell me.'

She hated how his lips brushed the outer shell of her ear.

'I'll lighten your soul,' he muttered. 'It's the adventure. I'll go first, if you want.'

And then he whispered his name into her ear – his full name – and finally pulled back, corpse-pale eyes glinting and slight playful smile tugging at the corner of his lips.

Reed's breath stuttered, and Pan let out a snort.

'Still won't tell me yours?'

The girl clenched her teeth and pressed her lips tight. She knew the fae stories.

But that simply made Pan grin more.

'Guess I'll just earn it the hard way,' he said with a light-hearted shrug. 'It's more of a game then. More rewarding when I finally get it.'

His face fell serious, which was somehow even more frightening than anything Reed had seen of this case yet.

'But, until then ...' he muttered.

Pan leant close again, pressing a long finger to her lips.

Reed wanted to pull away and scream, to wipe the touch from her mouth, but her body froze. She could do nothing but stare into his pale eyes – so pale they seemed like flame shining through murky water.

'Forget me not,' Pan whispered with a curling smile.

And then Reed's ears rang and her vision blackened over, and the world folded in on itself.

Until the blackness cleared and he'd gone.

Gone? How?

Reed blinked back to the world, still standing in the street with her feet glued to the spot like a spell had held her. And now she could finally move, yet it took a moment for her body to believe that was true.

A flush ran through her body, and she crouched and stared at the damp stone beneath her feet while her brain ran over everything that just happened.

Until—

She let out a little closed-mouth scream and wiped her mouth roughly on the back of her coat, not caring if she rubbed them raw until they bled.

He touched me! she cried to herself. *He actually touched me. My face. My lips!*

Reed shuddered – a whole body rejection that turned her stomach, and no matter what she did or how much she scrubbed, she could still feel his lingering touch on her lips.

How disturbingly soft his fingers had been.

And how that had made it feel all the worse.

She turned on the spot and marched back towards Devitt's house, glaring at the air in front of her.

I'll eat too hot, overcooked food every day until I die if I need to, she thought, curling her hands into fists. *Anything to burn this feeling away.*

As if it would ever go away. And nor the itching feeling in her blood.

Without knowing why, she reached into her pocket. Grabbed her notebook and her pencil. Scratched notes down as quickly as she could before remembering, all of a sudden, about Alice.

She paused mid stride.

Alice!

How had she forgotten? She'd just left Martha and Alice huddled on the floor, shaken. Alone. Without explanation. And she'd just run off.

They must have been so scared.

And no one else knew about this. Someone had to tell Scotland Yard.

But that was her.

She ran back to the house. Tore back up the steps. Crashed back through into Alice's room and breathlessly crashed to her knees in front of Martha, who still rocked a teary-eyed Alice in her lap.

'I'll send for him,' Reed gasped. 'Get Devitt back, I mean.'

Martha looked as if there was something else she wanted to say for a moment, but then she shut her mouth and simply nodded, returning to stroking Alice's yellow hair.

'Thank you,' Martha whispered as Reed rose and left.

And it echoed in Reed's head the whole night.

While she rushed back to the station. While she passed on the news. While she was dismissed back to her home – not allowed to wait for Devitt's return or to hear what happened next. And it echoed still as she collapsed into her mattress squashed between two other girls in a crowded shared room, and despite everything, her body succumbed to the darkness and she slept.

Dreamt of a feather and a girl with yellow hair flowing in the wind.

Falling.

She awoke with a start as the floor crashed beneath the yellow-haired girl, and sunlight pierced Reed's overtired, sensitive eyes.

She flinched and rolled over. Stared at the empty bedding next to her while her mind tortured her over everything she'd seen the night before.

It had been so real. So close.

Too close.

And she'd seen Pan. *Spoken* to him.

But for the life of her, she couldn't remember what they'd spoken about.

She glared at her room-mate's pillow.

It was all muddled in her head. Pan's voice was cloudy, muffled. Breaking. But his eyes – those creepy, corpse-grey, still-water eyes – ever watched her. Stared. Taunted. Unblinking with a hidden laugh behind them.

And the curl of his lips as he'd touched his finger to hers ...

Reed pushed her face into her lumpy pillow and screamed, then leapt to the corner. Grabbed her rag of a hand towel and a shared sliver of yellow soap and scrubbed her lips over a pail of water until her lips were raw and bitter.

But at least the pain covered that feeling he'd left.

She didn't care that she returned to the chaotic station that morning with her lips chapped and stinging. That's how her soul felt anyway as people rushed about her and ignored her, all panicked and yelling about the missed attack at Devitt's house.

And about how another pair of children had jumped that night.

Reed froze amongst it all, watching everyone bustling and pushing around her.

Another household.

Another lullaby.

And that itching feeling in her blood returned to realise that as soon as Pan had talked with her – smiled at her, *touched* her, been *seen* by her – he'd gone straight to another house and set more children for flight.

As if it were merely a game, and that her achievement of finding him had been nothing after all.

10

The Boy Who Refused to Grow Up

Devitt

Devitt sat at the foot of his daughter's bed, watching the slow and reassuring rise of her chest. He let out a shaky breath. Brushed a yellow curl back behind her ear. Here she was, sleeping peacefully, as if nothing had happened the night before.

As if she hadn't just nearly jumped to her death, lured by a boy who believed in faeries.

Devitt leant over. Pressed his forehead to his daughter's, then gave her a scratchy peck on the top of her head before padding down the steps to the kitchen.

To where Martha sat at the old wooden table, hands hugging a clay mug of weak tea.

He paused in the doorway. Locked eyes with his wife, and they both sighed.

'How is she?' Martha asked, voice quiet.

Devitt rubbed a hand over his chin. Stubble had become a short beard since he'd last been home, and he wasn't certain he liked it.

He moved to join her at the table – opposite, where he'd placed his own tea earlier.

'Finally asleep,' he muttered.

He let his feet drift across the space between them, finding her ankles then linking them with his own. A small touch. An *I'm here* when there was nothing better.

Just a silent gaze across the table as they both tried to fill a gap that they had no way to fill. Because how could you fill that silence when you'd nearly lost so much?

'The other kids?' Martha whispered.

Devitt watched as she stared into her own cup now, no doubt feeling the same guilt that lodged in his chest.

That other children had died when their own had been miraculously saved.

'Senator Hall's kids,' he said, taking a sip of the now lukewarm tea. 'Both of them.'

Martha's mouth trembled.

'Not your fault,' he added quickly. Took a great gulp of his tea this time. Reached across the table and took Martha's hand in his. 'Not yours. *His*.'

Martha looked back up at him. 'This is why you've been away this whole time?'

Her voice cracked in the way he hated. Hated how it pierced him right where it *should*. His heart and soul. Reminding him he was betraying his vows to her. To be here. To look after the family.

And he so wanted to be here. Both Heaven and Hell knew it. And he hated when he was torn away.

But this case ...

Devitt shifted in his seat. Stared about the sparse room. Tried to figure out how you told someone all of *this*. The children. The threats.

Devitt sighed. Leant back in his chair.

'We had it all wrong,' he admitted, tilting his head to the side and staring at his cup. 'We thought he was going after *him*.' He paused to think back to it all. 'The politician. Beechworth. He threatened us.'

'Politicians,' Martha snapped, with such distaste it made Devitt look up.

She shrugged, and Devitt could only nod.

'It was our assistant who realised,' he said. 'That he was going after kids. But no one listened.' And he frowned. 'Not even me.'

'The girl who came here?'

Devitt nodded, but couldn't bring himself to look at Martha now. He covered his face with his hands and cried out with a realisation that could swallow the whole of London.

He hadn't listened. And if it hadn't been for Reed acting anyway, his own daughter would have—

'Thank goodness she did,' Martha breathed.

Devitt knew it would be chaos after Senator Hall's kids were found dead in their garden. The concept that they'd have jumped themselves being the worst-taken aspect, no matter how much Devitt tried to explain they'd been manipulated to do so. And that Reed had seen the culprit was of no concern of the politicians.

An assistant – a *girl*, no less – having a say?

It drove Devitt mad.

And with Beechworth and the higher-ups storming into the station and demanding an audience with himself and the commissioner, taking up precious time Devitt could be using on solving the case, his patience was wearing thin. Particularly as Beechworth seemed to have forgotten that it was *his* doing that had Devitt and Scotland Yard teams posted outside his house for a night watch, rather than letting them continue the investigation elsewhere.

'Someone's clearly after the children of the leaders of London,' Beechworth told the crowding media in the doorway of the station as he marched out of the morning meeting. 'Thinking they can control us with violence. Well, I say it *won't* happen.'

Devitt hung back and watched the media drink it all in, knowing Chattoway must've been milking every moment of this. Onlookers roared questions over one another, and pencils scratched on tattered pocket notebooks – no doubt to be exaggerated and printed in that night's newspapers. By morning, there wouldn't be a street corner that didn't have the newsboys crowing about it. It would follow in his footsteps from here on.

He grit his teeth.

Not just the kids of London's leaders, he thought.

Going by what Reed had said of her days on the streets, kids had been disappearing like this for a long time. And those reports they'd found recently – the child that had supposedly died falling from their window from 'sleepwalking'.

The child of a baker.

It wasn't just the children of the rich, though of course those would be the ones people actually cared about. Reported. Spoke about.

No one would care enough about the others to even mention it as an issue.

The city was shaken. Finally they cared enough to open their eyes. And it took a few rich children after years of others dying for anyone to notice.

Devitt couldn't help but wonder whether that was what Pan wanted.

He turned and left the bellowing crowd of media to interview the politicians on their doorstep. Chattoway could handle it. Instead, Devitt sought out the cramped corner at the edge of the station, where a small black-haired girl hunched over files in weak lamplight with the focus of someone obsessed.

She didn't notice the first few times he called her name.

'Oy,' he kicked the leg of her broken chair. She startled and caught herself as it wobbled. 'Reed.'

She blinked up at him a few times before registering it was him, then promptly rose with a start and was suddenly far more formal than she'd been for a while, saluting with a quick 'sir'.

Devitt wrinkled his brow and stared at her face. 'What happened to your mouth?'

The young woman curled her lip and looked away. 'Pan.'

'He attacked you?'

She shot him a look of surprise. Then, 'Not exactly.'

But her tone told him to end it there, and so he did. Instead, he leant against a cabinet. Watched as she pretended to busy herself with more old reports of dead or missing children.

'You're the one who saw it first,' he said finally. 'I should've listened properly. Earlier.'

She finally looked up. Eyes roamed the wall behind him as if she was searching for something to say in response.

'I want you to keep helping me on this,' he said. 'Forget what the commissioner said. You're doing good.'

Reed met his gaze again. Wary, like she couldn't truly believe him.

'I found a kid,' Reed said slowly.

Devitt's heart snapped for a moment, and he straightened up instantly.

'From St Jude's, I mean,' she added quickly. 'He'll talk to us. Knew Pan.'

'When was this?'

'This morning,' she said. 'I was doing a bit of digging while you were stuck with Beechworth but ... didn't think it would help much.'

The cabinet Devitt leant against rocked back as he instantly pushed himself off it. 'It'll help!' he cried, then pushed on his hat and wove around her desk to leave. 'At this stage, anything will help.'

There was a clatter as she rushed off her chair to follow and it fell to the floor. 'But you have to buy him a hot meat pie if you want him to tell you anything,' she called after him as they left the station. 'That was the deal he made me agree to.'

Reed threw on her coat and took Devitt down increasingly tightening alleyways until they arrived at a dank and broken building by the side of a row of old markets along the Thames. How she even knew of such a place, or had found someone here, Devitt would never know. But before long she was snapping at a huddle of street kids to *scat*, leaving just one remaining.

A boy of about fifteen, Devitt guessed. Slim and with a darting look in his eyes as they glared out over the moth-eaten dark green scarf he'd wrapped around his neck and lower face an impossible number of times.

Devitt pulled one of the three hot meat pies he'd bought from his pockets and held it out to the boy. Instantly, the boy's brows rose, and he glanced over at Reed.

'As agreed,' she said, straightening her back.

The boy slipped forwards and took it, instantly retreating to open it in a place Devitt couldn't grab it back off him. Sat on an old crate Devitt was sure would collapse under him. Within no time, the newspaper wrapper was torn off, the scarf was pulled down, and the boy was stuffing the pie into his mouth.

'Oy, you too,' Devitt muttered, nudging Reed with his elbow while she watched the boy. 'We may as well eat too.'

Her eyes widened, but she took it, and the two sat to join the boy.

'We get locked out in the day,' the boy said between large mouthfuls, spitting pastry and crumbs of meat into his lap as he spoke. 'Can go wherever we want, so long as we're back at dark.'

He licked his fingers between mouthfuls.

'It's true Matron keeps his old door locked.' And then he laughed. 'Everyone's right scared. Some of the lads tried taking his old room for themselves, but they got scared when bad stuff started happenin' to 'em.'

In no time, the pie was gone. Devitt stared in awe as the boy wiped his mouth on his sleeve and brushed his dirty fingers down his trouser legs. Meanwhile, Devitt was barely a bite into his, struggling to keep it down what with a particularly strong and unpleasant sewage smell wafting from the river nearby.

'Said they heard pipes 'n' singin' 'n' stuff. Then one of the lads jumped from the window and Matron got scared. Locked it up.'

'What happened to the boy who jumped?' Reed asked. Somehow, she'd already finished her pie too, and was now casually leaning back and scanning the buildings around them when she wasn't shooting watchful glances back at the boy.

The boy shrugged. 'Dead, innie.'

Reed gave a soft 'Oh' that Devitt thought seriously underplayed the truth of it.

'That was just after Pan left, though. I reckon it was coz he didn't give his proper offerings, like.'

'Offerings?'

'Yeah, we were meant to bring things to him. Even now, actually.'

'Why?' Reed asked.

'Because bad things happen if we don't. Like him who jumped from that window. It was his own fault, really, weren't it.'

Devitt curled his lip. Needed the boy to keep talking so kept his own mouth shut. Instead, he inspected the inside of his pie. Tried to figure out what meat they'd used and why it tasted so odd. Eventually, he decided he wasn't sure he wanted to know after all.

'What was it like back then?' he asked the boy. 'St Jude's, I mean. When Pan was there.'

The boy leant back on an old crate and stared up at the sky as he thought, pulling his scarf back up over his chin. Picture of innocence, though Devitt highly doubted it was true.

'Less stiff,' he said finally. 'I mean, it's always stiff. The matrons are well tough. But when Pan was there, it was always chaotic. He didn't listen well. Always ignored the adults and said he would never grow up. Told fun stories. Made up things. He was a weird sort, but he made it more bearable.' The boy looked back down at them and shrugged. 'I dunno where he went in the day. We all go our own way and he didn't like behind followed. Went into the local forests. Told us fancy stories about crossing rivers, entering goblin doors and faerie circles. You know, old things. We didn't really believe it, but it was a bit more fun than God's death and damnation that Matron always bangs on about.'

Reed let out a scoff but tried to hide it as a cough. The boy grinned at her.

'Was weird though,' the boy added. 'He was a friendly fellow. Always talked to the new kids. Made them give him their name as soon as they turned up. But it was like they were under his control after that. Now and then he'd let kids go to the forest with him. Chosen ones, like. But they came back ... different.'

He scrunched his face up as he tried to think and tilted his head. 'You know ...' He searched their faces for help expressing his thoughts, but Devitt had no idea how to chip in.

'Well, I'm not sure. But they were different. Believe me.'

'We do,' Devitt found himself saying.

The boy smiled.

'Other kids got feathers in their beds. Spoke of adventures. Of flying. Somehow, they were always happy.' he frowned and kicked a stone on the ground. 'Dunno how. Ain't nuthin' happy about St Jude's, is there?'

Devitt tilted his dead to nudge the boy on.

'They were well lucky. I wish I could've been picked to go with him on an adventure. Anything's better than St Jude's.'

'You mean a trip to the forest?' Reed asked.

The boy shook his head. 'Nah. The proper ones. Pirates and mermaids and the like. Another land. Another place.' His dark eyes searched theirs for understanding and agreement. 'Anywhere but here. Said something about a star.'

He shuffled. Seemed more coy or like he was trying to act uncaring.

'Second star to the right of the moon,' he mumbled.

The phrase made Devitt's skin fizzle. The chalk stars. Half of them were a constellation of three. A perfect crescent moon. Two stars to the right.

The second one circled.

So it was a map? A message?

The boy shrugged and gave a dramatic sigh like he was trying to clear it all out. Like he didn't care. 'But, I never got picked. Only the special kids got to go.'

'Picked for what?' Reed said, her voice hurried. Pushing.

'To join the Lost Boys.' His eyes met Devitt's again. 'His gang. Believe me, mister. They were cool.'

'What happened to them?' Devitt asked. 'You can't join now?'

The boy shook his head. 'Nah. They disappeared when Pan left. All left together, I think. But we heard the stories.'

'What stories?'

He smiled faintly. 'You know, the adventures. Flying. How they reached the other land. Made it away from here. Finally.'

His eyes roamed back to Devitt's pie – Devitt had been so focused on the story he'd left it half untouched. And that strange discomfort of being watched etched at him so much he sighed and held out the rest of the pie for the boy.

'Here.'

The word had barely left his lips before the boy grabbed it with a grin. Scoffed the last of the pie so quickly Devitt would believe it if the boy ate the newspaper wrapper next.

'That everythin', mister?'

Devitt glanced over at Reed. She shrugged. So he sighed and ran a hand through his hair and gave a slow nod. 'I think that's everything.'

'Great!'

And the boy balled up the newspaper wrapper and tossed it back to Devitt before he promptly turned and strolled away with a cheerful wave, whistling as he went.

Devitt winced.

Whistling *that* lullaby.

'Do all the kids at St Jude's know it?' he grumbled as he and Reed turned to head back to the station.

Reed strained to look back at the boy as he walked along the river's edge. 'Probably,' she said. 'Sounds like Pan had quite the impact there. Important.'

'Too much,' Devitt said. 'Almost like he fancies himself as some sort of fae king,' he added quietly, feeling almost ridiculous for saying it aloud.

Reed looked up at him for a moment with a scrunched up face – the kind she always made when she was trying to read him inside-out. Then, after a moment: 'You make it sound like he's not really human,' she snorted, and her face lightened again.

'I think he used to be,' Devitt said, seriously now, scanning the decrepit buildings. Old police habit. 'But belief's a dangerous thing. Especially when no one stops it.' He looked down at her then and raised his brows. 'Can lead to anything.'

She stared dead ahead. Nodded. 'I wonder what happened to those "Lost Boys" though.'

11

Skipping Songs

Reed

Faerie circles and flying children. A magical land far away with mermaids and pirates and adventure?

Reed stomped harder through the streets, dodging a puddle and a pickpocket at the same time. Shoved her hands further into her oversized coat's pockets to cover up the few coins she owned.

Nonsense. Ridiculous. And children all around her actually believed it? Were dying for it?

For a boy who played creepy music for them and left them feathers and chalk stars?

She paused and stared in the window of a nearby bakery, staring at the fresh-baked bread. The smell taunted her and haunted all her senses. It would haunt her all day.

If only Devitt hadn't bought her that pie. After the taste of a fresh-baked hot meal, now she hungered for more. It would take her ages to forget about it and get used to her usual cold and tasteless scraps.

Her reflection in the bakery window caught her attention, and she stared. She was doing a little better than back then ...

The days on the streets. When they had nothing but each other, and pretty words and stories would keep them all going. Perhaps, then, stories of adventure would have worked more for her. So of course she knew why the street children fell for it.

When life was cold, wet, grey, and the cold seeped so deep even your bones shivered and your lips near froze together and you stared in shop windows like this with never a hope of even tasting a crumb ... Of course flying away to a magical land of mermaids and laughter and life would grab you.

You'd do anything for it.

So if a boy who thought he was a faerie said he could save you. Take you away from it all to somewhere better.

If you just had faith in him ...

She let out a shaky exhale. Remembered how persuasive he'd sounded that night. The smile.

But then the cold, corpse eyes and the way his finger had brushed her lips.

She shuddered and rubbed her mouth with her coarse coat sleeve again.

But the rich kids? The ones who had everything? Why would they risk it all?

The reflection of a street kid behind her caught her attention. Reed's eyes flickered from the bread inside to the yearning expression on the girl's little face before she was dragged away by an older kid in rags, neck craning to keep looking back at the baked goods.

Reed gritted her teeth and bit back the sting in her eyes.

Too real. Too close. She'd fix it, somehow. Until then, these kids were being wrung out of their hope and taken away.

Killed.

Not just the Lost Boys. But the Lost Children.

Just like her friend. Like Alice nearly had been.

But with seemingly no pattern to this strange game, and Pan showing no clear preference for *who* he targeted, how could they even hope to find which child would be next?

Devitt

Reed was staring into the window of the bakery like a lost child, Devitt thought as he noticed her on the street near the station later that day. But as he strode closer, he realised she wasn't even looking at the bread, but entirely lost in thought.

'Penny for your thoughts?' he grunted as he stepped in beside her.

She jolted.

'Not like you to zone out on the streets,' he said.

She sniffed and turned away, walking towards the station entrance. 'I was thinking about the case,' she said, her voice sharp as ever.

'Haunts you, doesn't it.'

Reed hummed in agreement. 'That's exactly the word I'd use.'

Devitt let his eyes roam the chaos of the street. Noisy as ever, newspaper boys and hawking vendors competed for attention, their voices crowing louder just to be heard over one another. And under that, the constant hum of crowds chattering to one another as they wove through.

It'd be dizzying, if Devitt wasn't used to it. The streets of London were always like this.

And yet, cutting over it all, somehow, a strange and jaunty tune caught his attention.

He paused and looked around. A street kid was busking with an old accordion – a tad off tune – in a corner of the main square, singing a skipping song for a bunch of kids in rags who swung an old, knotted rope for each other.

The kids seemed happy, but Devitt's face fell as he listened closer. Paid attention to the words.

> '... *Three for the high-borns lured to fate,*
> *And four happens when the blind detective's late.*
> *Five's the two ...*'

'Devitt?'

'So eight little birds can all take flight.'

'Oy, Devitt?'

Reed had stepped in beside him again. Elbowed him.

He blinked and looked down at her. 'Did you hear that?'

She frowned. 'What?'

'The song?'

She shrugged. 'There's always kids singing here.'

'No, the words he was singing.'

She looked uneasily between him and the busking street kid. Stared.

'See, he's going again. Listen.'

One is the child who leapt too far,
Two for the ones who followed the star.
Three for the high-borns lured to fate,
And four happens when the blind detective's late.
Five's the two with hands that won't let go,
Six in the circle drawn far below.
Seven is when the feather lands light,
So eight little birds can all take flight.
Nine is the door that swings open wide,
And ten is the last place the lost ones hide.

Devitt shuddered.

'I've never heard that before,' Reed said, and even her voice was uncertain and shaken.

'It's too ...' Devitt stared. He couldn't form words for this.

'Too real? Too close?' Reed answered for him.

Devitt nodded. That was exactly it.

'Why do I feel that's all I'm getting at the moment?' Reed muttered. Stuffed her hands back in her pockets and turned away.

But Devitt held back. Waited to listen again.

Reed scuffed her boots as she turned to wait with him.

Then, 'It's a bloody map!' he growled, immediately turning, stomping towards the station. 'He's playing with us.'

'Of course he is,' Reed said as if it was that simple. And it was. 'He always was. Should've seen his face that night ...'

But Devitt had already taken the ancient steps three at a time and was too far away to hear what she said next. He raced towards his desk. Pulled open his drawers and hastily shuffled through them. Pulled out a map of London.

'Where'd you put those reports of the kids we found?' he asked as Reed caught up, breathless for running after him.

Reed stared at him with the look of a woman asking if he was seriously asking her such a question – he got it all the time from Martha, but for the life of him couldn't figure out why such a tiny girl was giving him that look in his own office.

She finally let out a quick exhale through her nose with all the attitude only teenagers could muster, and without breaking eye contact with him, reached down and picked up a bunch of papers directly in front of him on his desk and slapped them back down right where she'd picked them up from.

Devitt blinked.

'Your desk's a joke,' she snapped.

But Devitt was already dropping into his seat and leafing through them, too busy to care for the attitude.

'So this is my house,' Devitt said, circling it with pencil. 'And this is the Beechworth house.' He looked up at her. 'I'm guessing they're the three high-borns the song talked about?'

'The other two kids the other day were here,' Reed pointed.

Devitt marked it up. Sat back and stared at it. 'Four happens when the blind detective's late ...' he repeated quietly.

They fell silent.

'That's me,' he said, and fell forward, resting his elbows on the table and raking his fingers through his hair. 'I'm the blind detective.'

'But that was two kids over here,' Reed said, pointing where the senator's children died. 'Isn't that "Five's the two with the hands that won't let go' or whatever it was?"'

'I'm guessing Alice was meant to be *four*, if you hadn't got there first.'

Devitt sighed and straightened again. Circled where Reed's finger was. 'The senator's children jumped holding hands. Rigor mortis set in before we got there. We couldn't separate their hands.' He paused and stared unseeing at the map. 'I can't get it out of my head.'

He noticed how Reed's lip curled in disbelief. And then she pulled up a spare stool he kept crammed in a corner and sat heavily into it. Stared. 'Dark song, innit.'

Devitt would've said that was an understatement. But then, everything about Pan's game was just becoming darker and darker.

'But that only starts at three, then,' he said, leafing through the old reports. 'Who do you reckon were one and two? When did he start considering this his game?'

Reed shrugged. 'I'm wondering about "six",' she said, leaning over and looking at the map. 'Six in the circle drawn far below. Does that mean there are going to be six next?'

Devitt groaned. He hoped not. Stared at the map.

There was no circle on here. Not yet.

'He always circles one of his stars in the chalk drawings,' Reed added hopefully. 'Maybe it makes one of those patterns?'

Try as he might, Devitt couldn't connect the three marks they had so far.

'Mark these up first,' Reed said, flicking through a couple of the old reports and pointing to where one of the earlier kids had been found. 'Maybe they'll help too.'

They marked two more deaths up – the two closest to the date of the Beechworths, hoping they'd be the first two in the song they'd missed.

'They make a star,' Devitt said, wondering if this was some kind of joke.

'Of course they bloody do,' Reed tutted. 'He's obsessed.'

'Reckon he'll circle around it next?' Devitt said half to himself. 'We've got five points for a star. Now's the circle?' He looked up at her. 'You mentioned there's always a circle around one of the chalk stars.'

Reed shrugged. 'Worth a shot.'

He drew a circle connecting the five points together. They both bent over the map and stared.

'Does that mean the next kid can be anywhere on this line?'

Devitt repeated the next line of the song in his head. 'Six …' He slumped back into his chair. 'Does that mean one child is the sixth in this game, or six children?'

It clawed at his chest to even say it. Both were equally horrifying. But to think there might be *six* victims next …

Reed glared at the map as if the circle would give up and tell them the answer if she scared it enough. He wished she'd say something. Fill in the silence he didn't know how to fill. Because when it got this quiet, he swore he could hear that boy out on the street singing that song again.

The horror he'd felt sank to his stomach. And then, the accordion began the little tune again, and Devitt burst up from his chair.

'Come with me a moment,' he muttered, rushing out of the room.

He went straight for the busking street kid. Stopped in his tracks as he reached the skipping children, and the song abruptly stopped as the kids stared at the detective frozen in front of them.

A feather had been placed in the boy's coin collection hat since Devitt had last stood there. His heart pounded and his mouth dried up so much that when he tried to speak, it came out croaked.

'Where'd you learn that cheerful tune, now, lad?' he asked, tossing a coin in the hat, trying to be as light as he could, despite how his insides were begging to be dragged up from the icy depths of the Thames.

The boy grinned as the coin clunked against the stone beneath his thin hat.

'An older boy taught me!' he crowed. Thumbed towards his own chest proudly. 'Learnt it in a single night, I did.'

'Didja now?' Devitt said, trying to keep his voice soft. 'Very good of you.'

Behind him, Reed finally caught up, scowling at him and grumbling about having to apologise for him to a constable he'd barged into on the way out.

Devitt hadn't even noticed.

'Yeah, it's good, isn't it. Goes so well on my accordion.' He stretched out his instrument. Played a few chords. 'Want to hear it again?'

But it was the kids who'd been skipping who answered. Begged him to play again. And so Devitt took a step back to give space for the kids to play, and he watched with amazement as they so happily skipped to such a dark song.

Did they not understand it?

He looked down at the hat again. Only a few coins were inside, next to that feather.

And then he blinked. Next to the hat was that same drawing again. A crescent moon and two stars. The second star circled, with a smiling face inside.

'There it is again,' he muttered to Reed as he stepped back to stand beside her. 'Know anything about the old faerie stories?'

She shook her head. 'But there's an old ley line map on the wall in the library's archives. Saw it when I snuck in to hide from the cold once.'

'You think I give a damn about ley lines?'

Reed glared up at him. 'No,' she said, weighted. 'But I think *he* does. If he thinks he's a bloody fae king wearing leaf crowns and drawing chalk stars everywhere and crossing goblin doors and telling everyone about visiting different worlds ...'

She paused and thumbed in the direction of the library.

'He's playing by fae rules,' Reed continued. 'Maybe we should, too.'

And, oh, Devitt hated how that ley line map lined up exactly with where the street boy had been playing. He held their map up in front of it while Reed marked where the library's copy showed the ley lines.

'The ley lines cross our circle here, here, here, and here,' Reed said, pointing to them as Devitt placed their notes down on a nearby table.

They both looked up at one another.

Devitt nearly swore.

'Which is next?' she asked, her eyes sharp.

He rubbed both his hands down his face. Wanted to claw at himself. Get his brain working. Stop all this nonsense about fae and stars and feathers and dreams and go back to dealing with the real world again.

Not that that wasn't any more messed up.

'We have no way to know, and I'm inclined to say all of them.'

Reed's mouth dropped open a little. 'But how do we deal with that?'

Devitt straightened up. Folded his map again and stared at the ley line guide on the library archive's wall. Four major points.

'We'll send people to each of them.'

'Will the commissioner listen?' Reed asked.

Devitt didn't blame her for her doubt. The commissioner was the sort who never believed in things that didn't have real force or facts. But Devitt wasn't going to risk another child this time.

'Leave it to me,' he said, shoving his map into his coat's inner pocket.

The accordion boy was still playing when they walked back to the station. But by now, the other kids had stopped skipping, and he stood alone.

'Eight is the moment they all take flight.'

12

The Children on the Line

Devitt

The police carriages fanned out just before dusk, shortly after Devitt had thrust the map in front of the police commissioner's eyes and convinced him the pattern had been deciphered.

Now, icy water leapt up Devitt's leg as he stomped through the darkening streets, puddles and all. A station carriage had just dropped him and a couple of constable supports to the area the ley line crossed Pan's circle. But what that map couldn't tell them was which house Pan was targeting.

There were a few.

So, with no idea when the victim might jump or from where, he and the other constables split up to check every gateway and window for signs of chalk stars, feathers, and dazed, smiling children.

Devitt cursed. And this was just one of the four points on the star. This would be happening at each of the points Reed and the other detectives and constables in the station had visited, to save the victims of the deranged child that played this game.

A shudder shot through his body.

By now, the night fog was rolling in, and Devitt shrugged his coat closer, squinting through the grey haze.

Of course, this only made it harder.

Reed

Reed leapt from the carriage before it had even fully stopped. Her heart was lodged in her throat, and something was screaming at her to move.

Now.

And the pressure of having the police commissioner right behind her didn't help, either.

He'd seen the map. Had identified the group of houses where two of the ley lines met as where his nieces lived and was now entirely convinced they'd be the ones at risk.

And knowing the game Pan had them all playing, it could very well have been the case.

But this meant Reed strained against the invisible lead she felt tied to, trying to rush ahead to the aid of the children, desperate to save them, but limited to staying behind the commissioner.

As was her place.

To give him credit, the man moved quickly. But years of being behind a desk meant that wasn't quick enough for Reed.

Come on, they're going to die! she begged over and over in her head.

Her frantic energy had her scanning the area with her eyes. If she couldn't rush on ahead, she'd stalk the area from here.

She paused. Squinted into the darkness.

Chalk lines scraped across the entire street. Down walls, over the gate, down the footpath, right to where the police commissioner had said his sister's house was.

She let out a small, almost impressed exhale. His instincts had been right.

The man finally dashed forwards at a pace Reed could cope better with. And as they followed the chalk line closer to the house, on the brick wall beside the gate were white chalk stars.

One with a smile in the middle.

But that wasn't all. There, on the top floor at the front window, two sisters were climbing onto the windowsill, humming that same haunting song to one another and waving feathers as if they were wings, giggling.

Eyes so glazed they didn't even notice their uncle and his police team below.

Devitt

With the eerie night as it was, Devitt half expected to hear that lilting pipe song again. Didn't it happen each time the children leapt? Wasn't that their cue? Constable Harrow had said he'd heard it the night the Beechworth children had been found, but Devitt hadn't been present at the other events to know, and he'd missed his opportunity to ask Reed before she left with the commissioner's team.

He should have asked her. Because now he was straining to listen to the wind, begging the night for a clue.

Who would leap, from where, and when?

Or was this just another sick distraction? Like the night they'd got it wrong about Beechworth, and children were falling to their deaths this very moment somewhere else, hoping to fly to some magical other world where things would be better.

Devitt gritted his teeth and ran back the way he'd come. He'd strayed too far from the area they'd marked up on the map. Too far from where the circle crossed the ley line.

That only meant three or four houses.

He froze as something crunched under his foot.

Looked down. Raised his foot.

A crunch of broken white crumbled rock and powder marked a splodge where he'd stepped.

Chalk.

His blood pounded and his mouth dried instantly as he spun on the spot, eyes taking in every inch of this place, hard as it was in the foggy darkness.

A line of white crossed the road right in front of him. Marked up the garden wall to his left. Stars sprinkled the wall near the front gate, a smile in the centre of one goading him.

Taunting him for not noticing.

The blind detective who'd failed to see the giant white circle drawn out this whole time, right under his very nose.

He tugged at the small tin whistle around his neck and sounded for the other constables to meet him. Followed the chalk forwards.

It was scuffed and fading in most places. Of course he'd missed it. But as he looked back up the trail towards where he'd identified the ley line, it led into one house.

The same one with all the stars on the wall by the gate.

Boots stomped and splashed closer, but his racing heart couldn't wait. His body urged him through the creaking metal entry, eyes desperately roaming every window he could see.

Nothing.

'Are they out back?' a voice behind him puffed as they caught their breath.

Devitt's lip curled as he scanned the row of townhouses. Long. Running the entire length of the street with no easy way to get to the back without running through the house.

That made things harder.

Reed

The young assistant didn't wait for the commissioner's instructions. She left him waiting in the garden, trying to call out to the girls and reason with them to go back inside.

But of course they wouldn't. Not with their minds swept like they were. Blank and controlled by dreams and songs from an eerie boy who'd told them they could fly.

Reed remembered the blank buzzing in her head that day he'd spoken to her. How easily he'd persuaded her to listen to his voice and look up.

The girls were long gone.

She and another constable swung through the wrought-iron gate and pounded the neat stone slabs towards the house.

'Forget the door!' she shrieked at the other constable just as he was reaching out for the bronze knocker.

There was thick ivy growing smartly up the side of the house, so Reed pointed towards it and leapt on. Hefted her way up. She could climb quicker than waiting for someone to open the front door. And no doubt the sister of the police commissioner would be well versed in keeping her front door locked.

There'd be no easy breaking in like at Devitt's house.

The girls giggled and sang above her, and Reed's only saving grace was the younger one moaning about the cold and turning to look back into the room. Asking her older sister whether she needed to go and fetch her coat, or whether *Neverland* was warmer.

'Of course it is,' the older sister said in a sing-song voice. 'It's beautiful sun every day!'

If only, Reed grunted to herself as she pulled herself up past the second floor. Sunny weather every day sounded far too good to be true.

Behind her, the commissioner was still standing in the garden, calling out to the girls. Below, the constable was struggling up the vine by the first floor, and the front door finally clicked open.

A scream made Reed wince.

She glanced down. The children's mother was staring up from the front door at her girls, and the nanny behind her gasped and immediately ran back into the house.

Reed hoped she had the common sense to run up and grab them from inside the nursery.

'Come on,' the older sister's impatience nudged through her voice, eager to go. She pulled at the younger sister's hand. 'Don't worry about a coat. Let's go. The feather said it's time. The song will start soon.'

'I'm scared!' the youngest whined. 'What if I can't fly like he said I can?'

Yes, listen to her! Reed grunted, her arms burning now. Slowing her down.

'It's okay,' the eldest said.

And from her vine, Reed shook her head. *No, no, no. Not yet.* She was nearly there. But the vine bit at her hands, and her weight was already easing the thick wooden branches from the wall. She could feel it pulling away. Jolting.

She looked up. But it was just a little further.

'Remember, all you need is faith in him. Trust him, and what else?' the older sister kindly prompted.

'And think of happy things,' the youngest finished with a bolder voice. 'Like Mama!'

The mother screamed out again below. Begged them. But of course that wouldn't work now. The girls giggled and the eldest started humming again.

Reed grunted with a final effort, finally just below them. She stretched out her arm. Tried to pin one of the girls' ankles or push them back into the nursery.

But the girls linked their fingers and stepped over her reaching hand.

And leapt.

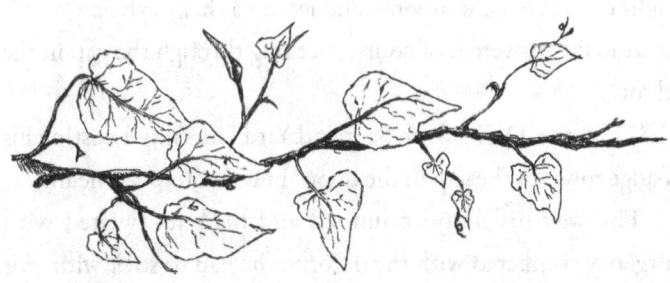

Devitt

How did one knock on the door of a house of people clearly wealthier than you, at night, and tell them you believe an orphan boy who thinks he's a faerie king has poisoned the mind of your child to lure them into leaping from their own bedroom window, believing they can fly to a new, magical world. And could he please come in to check and save the child.

Devitt had no clue, and yet he had to.

With no sign of feather nor child on this side of the house, they had to check the back windows, which meant passing through the house.

And so Devitt brushed past one of the constables and rapped on the silver door knocker – so shiny it had a sheen even in the light of the crescent moon – and let out a shaky exhale.

A maid answered, of course, peeking through the gap in the door.

'Detective Devitt from Scotland Yard,' he said, thrusting his badge towards the gap in the door. 'I need you to let me in.'

The way his blood pounded and his guts twisted with urgency conflicted with the decorum he had to stick with. For the job. But he desperately wanted to tear past her and rush up to the nursery to find the child – or children.

The maid stared at the badge, and Devitt's entire body vibrated at how slow he could see her brain working.

'I need to enter,' he pressed. 'Where is your master?'

The maid paled as if she was the one in trouble, and it irked him. Devitt tutted and pushed past her, growling at one of the constables to explain to her. Then he bound up the steps inside the house, taking them two at a time, and slammed through every door, not caring who he disturbed.

The lady of the house shrieked as he threw open a door to a giant living room, where she'd been sewing. He barely shot her a second glance before he rushed out again.

The nursery wasn't on this floor. And somewhere outside, he swore he heard a pipe lullaby floating on the wind.

Devitt bound up the next set of stairs, urgency breaking him. His eyes near stung with frustrated tears at his own imagination playing out what would happen if he were to be late. If the child jumped before he found them.

The tune got louder as he reached the top floor.

Not pipes. Humming.

His heart smashed. The child was alive – still. In the room ahead. He'd got there in time. Maybe. But if the child was singing that tune, it wouldn't be much longer before ...

Devitt shook that image from his head and darted across the remaining hallway and barged into the nursery. A boy in neat clothes was sat on the windowsill, his back to the door.

The song stopped as the boy turned, gasping, and stared wide-eyed at Devitt.

In his hand was a large black feather.

'Who are you?'

Fear rang through the boy's voice, and he shuffled where he sat, almost trying to edge away from the presumed intruder.

But that was the worst thing he could have done. Devitt cried out as the boy wobbled on the windowsill, flailing his arms as he toppled sideways over the edge.

The detective lunged forwards. Crushed the boy's shoulders in his arms and hoisted him back over the ledge and into the room, ignoring the boy's cries of fear and pain. He placed the boy safely on the floor. Crashed to his knees, breath ragged. Watched the boy blinking back to full attention and stare around his own nursery.

He'd made it.

Reed

Reed screamed and lunged back, her free arm flailing. She'd been so close, she couldn't lose now.

Reaching out as far as she could, Reed tried to grasp at anything she could grab onto.

Caught fabric. Clenched.

Cried out as her fingers burnt at fabric slipping then catching in her grip, and an ache flushed through her arm and shoulder at a weight pulling her down the vine.

But somehow, she held. The fabric held. And she looked down to see her fingers twisting in the youngest daughter's nightgown belt.

She had her. Swinging like a spider and crying out in pain. But she had her.

But the eldest?

Slipped from the grip of their joined fingers.

Reed stared as the girl fell and cursed for not making it in time. A scream pierced from above – the nanny leaning through the window just above Reed's head.

They both watched in horror as the girl fell.

In a heartbeat, the constable on the vine below her launched himself from the wall. His arms opened wide, and he caught the girl in a protective embrace and he fell before her, roaring out with a bellow of pain as his back crashed into the garden floor beneath them instead of her tiny body.

Reed dangled there, shaking with effort, the younger girl sobbing in her grip.

Below, the constable groaned – alive, thank goodness – and checked the older sister in his arms as the childrens' mother and the commissioner both ran, yelling, towards him.

And somewhere, in the dark, Reed heard a single, lilting pipe note.

13

Where the Chalk Washes Away

Devitt

Devitt's boots were heavy when he got back to the station later that night. A mix of fatigue and shock and that twisted-stomach feeling you always get when guilt gnaws at you.

The kid had nearly fallen because of him. Because he'd shocked him.

But he's alive, he reminded himself.

The station was frantic. Teams were returning in clatterings of horse hooves and cart wheels, and voices called over one another to hear the news.

Devitt kept score. All four sites successful. All children saved. Six of them.

Six in the circle drawn far below.

He hated that it matched up to the song that well. Hated how Pan played with that many lives all at once.

Reed slumped on her chair in her little corner, and Devitt pushed through everyone to check on her. She straightened as she saw him approach.

Her face was paler and peakier than ever, with dark shadows etching under her eyes.

'Heard you got to both kids in time,' Devitt said. 'Good job.'

But the young girl flinched.

'Nearly didn't,' she said, her gaze slipping to look anywhere but at him. 'Jumped right over me, they did. And I only managed to catch one.'

She paused and twisted around to look back into the main room. 'That yellow-haired constable there actually caught the other just before she hit the ground.' Her dark eyes found his again, and she let out a shaky breath. 'Thought we'd failed her.'

Devitt let out a sigh that was half a darkness-accepting laugh.

'Yeah?' He tilted his head as he watched the self-judgement and self-loathing cross Reed's young face. 'Well, least you weren't the one to *cause* the child to jump.'

He'd meant it to joke and reassure her. And perhaps it did. She looked up at him with wide-mouthed, wide-eyed shock, and he snorted disparagingly.

'Boy leapt out of his skin when I crashed into his nursery. Was already sat on the windowsill. Leant back to get away from me and nearly toppled over.'

Reed's brows dug a ravine into her forehead. 'You made it sound like you pushed him.'

Devitt shrugged. 'We're all tired.'

She nodded and returned to staring at random files on her desk. It was too dark now to see properly, but he was certain she'd have memorised these by now.

'All pretty high profile, weren't they?' he said to ease the silence. 'Commissioner's nieces. Son of a high bishop. Child of one of the biggest industry bigwigs.' He counted them on his fingers. 'And the last two were even the kids from the French ambassador.'

'French ambassador?' Reed's face twisted up. 'Pan can speak *French*?'

Devitt couldn't help the snort that let lose then. 'I'd imagine the kids can speak English. Particularly if they're over here, visiting.'

She stared at him for a moment. Then looked away.

'So, six. Just like the song said.' And then she gasped. 'Wait. But you didn't mention the street musician. Wasn't he there too?'

Devitt frowned as he stared at her. And it took a moment too long for him to realise why the street musician would be relevant at all.

'He had a feather,' he whispered, disbelieving. Clawed a hand through his hair and turned on the spot to stare at the chaos of constables exhausted and trading stories in the main room. 'He had a feather!'

Then he turned back to her. 'But I spoke to everyone. He wasn't at any of the marks.'

Reed's chair toppled over as she leapt up.

'I'm going to find him,' she called over her shoulder as she pushed past him and wove through the noise of the station.

She was already halfway to the other side of the square by the time Devitt caught up with her, and when they skidded to a stop at the corner the boy with the accordion had been busking at earlier, there was no child there.

But then Devitt hadn't really expected him to still be standing there at this time of night.

'It's still early night,' he said, turning on the spot and looking around, wondering where the boy might go to sleep. 'We might still have time.'

'Don't count on it,' Reed cried, already darting off again down a too-dark alley.

Devitt wondered how she knew where to run, until a faint sound picked up over his boot steps.

Pan pipes – of course. Could she have heard that?

He gritted his teeth. Pan would have known they'd miss this one. Would be here to goad them. And perhaps Devitt only imagined the extra creepy, extra smug sounding lilt of that lullaby tonight.

And then, somewhere in the dark and the fog, the accordion responded, echoing the lullaby.

'This way!' Reed yelled, turning down a small alley that Devitt wouldn't have considered. The network of small alleyways and boxes on the side and strewn messes were places to avoid. You never knew what you would step in, or who would be there.

But they avoided the watching eyes of those who lay there, and only a child who knew the streets could ever have guided him through such a maze to follow a sound that also seemed to move.

Had he been alone, he'd have had no hope to find the boy.

'Sounds like it's coming from everywhere,' Devitt gasped, taking in great breaths of air as they stopped to choose a small turn.

'This one,' Reed said, running again, ducking under a twine washing line heavy with clothes.

Somewhere inside one of these close-knit buildings, someone was yelling. A man. And then Devitt winced at the sound of smashing clay and a scream.

Ahead of him, Reed barely flinched.

The accordion and pipes seemed almost beautiful in comparison, which was worrying.

'There!' Reed pointed, her voice lighter than it had been all evening. Triumphant, even. 'We can make it!'

But the accordion stopped then, and a small figure dropped down from a perch on a fence and turned to run.

Away from them. Back onto the main streets where late carriages wove in their way and street lamps burnt orange and bright almost mockingly after Devitt had finally learnt to see in the twisting backstreet mazes.

Devitt's heart shuffled and stuck in his throat. Was the boy running from them? Or to something?

'Wait!' Reed cried out, her arm reaching out as if she could grab the boy from the opposite side of a long street.

But the boy didn't wait, of course. He ducked behind a horse and down another street.

Devitt gritted his teeth and cried out as another carriage got in their way. Made them stop. And then, when they could finally turn the corner into another alleyway, it was to the sound of their own strangled cries as they nearly tripped over a small mangled and twisted body.

The detective gasped for air as his eyes roamed the scene. The boy's hat on the ground, narrowly missing a puddle of who-knew-what. The accordion lay stretched out and broken open like a cracked ribcage – much like, Devitt couldn't help but notice, the boy's own ribcage against the stone. And then, next to the boy's small and crooked form – eyes wide and dreamy, of course, with an unsettling smile on his face – was the feather.

Reed let out a loud, frustrated cry, and she kicked a loose stone down the alleyway.

'It's always us street kids who go forgotten,' she growled, shoving her hands in her pockets again. 'We should have been there for him! We saw the feather this morning.'

Devitt could only stare. What else could he say to that? She was right. But then ...

'He wasn't on the map,' he whispered, knowing it wouldn't help but couldn't for the life of him think of why. What it meant.

But then ... street kids didn't exactly have addresses. Nowhere permanent. How could he have been on the map?

'That doesn't *matter*!' Reed shrieked.

Devitt took a breath. Nodded. Tugged off his hat and held it to his chest as he stared back at the boy on the ground.

'I know,' was all he could say.

And somewhere above them, a pan pipe lullaby floated on the wind as Reed cried out every street curse she could recall at this deranged game, until her voice broke, and she just cried instead.

Until the music suddenly stopped.

14

The Faerie Star

Devitt

Reed crouched over the small twisted body of the street busker. Tears betrayed her, falling fast as she reached forward and gently closed his eyes.

She was a better person than him, Devitt thought. He who was unable to do anything but stand there and stare, trying to run the riddle over and over in his head and wonder where he'd gone wrong.

'We were too slow,' Reed hissed, leaning back on her heels. 'We let him win. We saw the feather earlier. We should have—'

Her voice cracked. She sniffed. Wiped her eyes angrily on her coat sleeve.

'We should have *been there* for him,' she finished.

And when Devitt had no reply, she continued, standing back up again. 'It's always the same. Always. It's always us who go ignored.' She stared at the boy. 'Forgotten.'

He heard her. Truly. But now?

Devitt let out a long breath and finally shifted. Walked a few paces. Stooped to pick up the broken accordion, wincing as it extended and wheezed in his grip, off-key and deranged now. Then, he stepped over to the boy's hat. Picked it up and dusted it off.

Reed watched him warily the whole time, her dark eyes narrowing.

Devitt crouched on the other side of the boy and placed his hat and accordion gently beside him. Looked at the boy. Then, he ran a great hand over his face and let out a low cry.

'He looks just like Martha's little brother.'

Reed

There was no way she could sleep tonight. Instead, Reed went straight back to the station, rushing immediately to her tiny, rickety desk in the corner and rifling through all her notes and reports.

Her eyes still burnt, and her throat had a dull ache from crying. And she hated that her heart couldn't stop pounding.

Devitt cleared his throat as he entered the small space. Leant on a cabinet and watched as she flicked through her notebook, desperate for any small clue that would help.

What was the next line of the skipping rhyme? Her head was caught in so many different directions she couldn't think. Would that have told them what would happen to the boy?

'Oh,' she breathed. 'It's here!'

Pan's name. The one he'd whispered to her that day before her ears had crashed and she'd forgotten it.

She'd drawn it in the book near the back, after so many blank pages. Why?

'What is?' Devitt prompted after a while of her simply staring at the page.

She blinked and looked up. Pointed to where she'd written – albeit it incredibly messily – a name. One she had no doubt was Pan's.

'His full name,' she told the detective. 'It's said if you give your full name, the old fae have control over you.'

'But why would he give you his name?'

Reed shrugged. 'Part of the game? Afterwards, I felt like he'd put a spell on me. I nearly fainted. Maybe he doesn't expect us to remember it.'

The detective frowned. 'Put a spell on you?'

Reed sighed. 'I know it's impossible, but it's how it felt.'

'I'm not saying that ...' Devitt started, standing straighter. 'But you just have it right there in that little book of yours?'

Reed nodded. Spun the book around so he could read it for himself. He scowled and looked back up at her. 'Think this will work against him?'

She had no idea how it would work. 'But surely it's worth the shot. It's all we have. And maybe we just need to make sure we use his full name before he takes ours.'

'Happen to know any other fae rules?' the detective asked her, lightly flicking through the paperwork on her desk – the reports on the other children.

'No,' Reed said. 'You?'

Devitt rubbed his chin and looked up at the dank ceiling. 'Only that they used to say you should never take gifts from them, and never pay more or less than you're due.' He met her gaze again with an expression like he barely believed it. 'Oh, and don't stray off common-made paths.'

Reed stared. 'But then how are they going to—'

Her eyes widened.

'Oh,' she breathed. 'Gifts.'

Devitt smiled then. 'The feathers? Aye, I just thought so too.'

'But what about the feathers and rocks and flowers and things the kids were leaving him at St Jude's?'

'Offerings, perhaps?' Devitt shuffled on his feet and crossed his arms. She watched as a frown bit a dent into the space between his brows. 'As their payments, perhaps?'

A cold wave shuddered down Reed's spine. 'Oh, he's so creepy.'

Devitt bowed his head. Stared at the paperwork on her desk again. Sighed.

'But payment for what?' Reed asked. 'And where's next?'

He reached into his pocket and pulled out the folded map they'd been using to track the children on the circle earlier.

Opened it and stared for a moment before stepping forward and laying it on her desk, on top of everything else.

'There, at the centre of it all,' Devitt said, pointing to a mark. 'Where the ley lines cross is *exactly* at the centre of the deranged star he'd drawn. Where he always draws that creepy smile in those chalk stars of his.' He looked at her. 'I bet that's where he is. He's drawn it all around himself.'

'Of course he did,' Reed muttered.

Devitt gave a small nod. 'Of course he did. And this time, I'm not waiting. It's still night. We have time now to get him while he's still acting.'

Reed sniffed and straightened in her wonky chair. Pushed down the anxiety that gnawed at her stomach like rats and bugs. 'Good,' she said. 'I'm coming.'

'No,' Devitt said, folding the map again and shoving it in his pocket. 'You're staying here. It's getting dangerous, and you should sleep.'

Reed swore at him. 'As if,' she said, rising from her chair. 'You heard the song, *blind detective*.'

Devitt winced, but she didn't care if that bit at him. She was still angry, and rightfully so. Or so she thought.

'I can look after myself,' she said. 'And no way will he try to take me. Knows I won't let him. And I certainly won't let him get away with this.'

Devitt sighed. Nodded. 'You'll only go alone if I say no, anyway, won't you?'

The defiant glare in her eyes said it all. She didn't need to nod, but she did anyway.

'Fine,' he grumbled, already turning to leave. 'But you stick close, and do what I say. And if this *Peter* gets too dangerous, I'm sending you away.' He jabbed a finger at her before she could protest. 'And that's an order.'

Reed nodded and hastily looked back in her notebook. Slammed it shut and pocketed it as she ran after him, repeating Pan's full name over and over under her breath.

This time, they'd win at the boy's own game.

Devitt

At the centre of the map's deranged faerie star was a crumbling warehouse. An old textile factory, that even from stepping outside it and staring at the towering mass of brick, Devitt swore he could hear the clack of machines and smell the wools, linens, and oils.

'Perfect place for a crim to hide,' Reed said, voice flat. 'It was always obvious *something* was going to happen here, if not him.'

Devitt could only agree.

'He makes it all so obvious,' she continued. 'Plays by all the stereotypes, at the end of it all. Once you know the rules.'

'Well,' Devitt shrugged. 'It's a game for him. I think he wants to be found.'

Reed sneered.

'I'm serious,' Devitt said, stepping forward again and rubbing his hands together against the night's chill. 'You're still new to this, but you'll be amazed at how many we catch that *want* to be found.'

He glanced back at her.

'Like it's some kind of acknowledgement,' he added. 'Someone finally seeing them.'

She frowned. 'Even for a bad thing?'

'If you're never seen, you'll do anything for someone to notice you, right?'

He heard her boot steps stop for a moment, and felt a sting where she was no doubt staring at him and trying to figure out whether she believed him. Then, her footsteps echoed in a fast trot to catch up.

'You're not wrong,' she said in a small voice. 'But we don't all want to do it that way. The bad way, I mean.'

He looked sidelong at her. Nodded.

'But our friend *Peter*, here,' he said, nodding to the building looming over them. 'Plays it like someone wrote a rulebook.' But then he smiled. Looked at her and earned a judgemental look back. 'Fae rules, eh? You know what they say about fae liking rules and rituals. That's how we'll win. There's rules in his game. He wants us to stick with them.'

Reed pouted. 'I hate rules.'

And Devitt couldn't help but chuckle. 'Don't we all. But that's where we'll win. We're not bound as tightly to them as he is.'

'Didn't think I'd hear that from a high up detective,' Reed teased. 'Thought police were bound by rules too?'

Devitt gave a light-hearted shrug. 'Sometimes rules need to be broken. For the greater common good.' He gestured ahead of them towards the warehouse with a lazy wave of his hand as they picked down the main entranceway. 'Especially when the rules are made by someone not following the rules of common society. He made them. Not us.'

They found the front door, earning Devitt a grumble from Reed about whether they were actually just going to waltz in through the front door.

'Why not?' Devitt said. 'He invited us.'

The young girl didn't look convinced.

'It's so obvious,' Devitt continued. 'On the map.'

He didn't wait for a response. Instead, he immediately pushed open the old door, the hinges so rusted he had to barge his shoulder against the door several times to get it to budge. Then, the hinges screamed as he hefted the door open.

'No need to knock when your door's that loud,' Reed tutted. 'Think he knows we're here?'

Devitt stepped through first, pausing in the doorway, looking around in the musty darkness within. 'Surely he must,' he muttered.

Behind him, Reed just sighed.

Inside, the warehouse was dark, but glints of light seeped through broken tiles and glass and danced off dust moats and old cotton balls that floated in the air. As the pair stepped further in, an echo of pan pipes etched that same old lilting lullaby into their hearts and bones, bouncing off the walls until it sounded like it could be coming from anywhere.

And, as their eyes finally adjusted to the darkness and they slowly stepped deeper, they found Peter standing at the dead centre – the grand warehouse room hollowed out of everything it had once held, now a mere shell.

The boy was staring right at them.

He removed the pipes from his lips and grinned. 'You came!'

The silence that followed the haunting pipe tune was just as eerie, Devitt thought. Just as foreboding. He almost wanted the tune to start up again – at least it would break this heavy weight. Instead, this silence felt like something would come crashing down on top of them.

But then, could silence even bring down a whole building? Right now, he believed it could.

'You caught six of my latest recruits,' Peter sang with a sigh. Then he stroked his pipes and looked down at them sadly. 'Missed the seventh, though, didn't you?'

Devitt could sense how Reed stiffened next to him. He gritted his own teeth, trying to hold back. To not spoil this by leaping too quickly. From where they were now, if Devitt even so much as tried to run and catch Peter, he knew the boy would have the upper hand to escape.

'Oh!' Peter said, tilting his head to look more at Reed standing slightly behind Devitt, as ordered. 'You brought one to me in return? What a lovely gift.'

Devitt stepped in front of the young girl and straightened to his full height. 'She's not for you.'

But behind him, Reed gasped, and Devitt whipped his head around to check on her.

'Look around you,' she muttered, stepping a little closer to him. 'It's them.'

Devitt furrowed a brow.

But Reed flicked her head for him to look ahead of him. 'The lost ones.'

And this time, when he turned and took in the scene some more, Devitt looked beyond Peter. At what else was in this hollow warehouse.

He forced his eyes to adjust further to the dim.

Of course the boy was standing in the centre of a damned fae circle. But this time, rather than drawing it with chalk, it had been built from bones.

Too many of them.

And not bird bones this time.

'They're human,' he whispered, unable to hold back his shock.

His eyes urgently roamed the scene some more, wondering what else he'd missed while his eyes were adjusting and his overly righteous head just focused on the boy. With it so dark, he tried taking in the smells instead.

Somewhere, beyond the old dust and fluff and linen and oil smells was something rancid and rotten.

A smell he knew all too well from so many years on the job.

Corpse.

'You'd have brought them here if we failed?' Devitt asked the boy, his voice cracking. 'Those kids from tonight.'

Peter frowned. Looked around him. 'Where else would they go?'

'Neverland?' Reed spat, leaning around Devitt. 'That's what you tell them, isn't it? Where they'll go if they jump.'

Peter smiled again. 'Neverland will come,' he said, voice dreamy. 'When the door opens. And they are the key.'

When neither Reed nor Devitt answered him, the pale boy shrugged and continued. 'How about you?'

Devitt noticed his focus was now entirely on Reed.

'Do you want to go where the stars sing?' Pan spun grandly in the centre of his circle, hands flung wide and head tilted back. 'There's a place beyond the black where no one grows old. Only lighter. Only freer.'

He stopped spinning and lowered his head to look at them, smile only somehow bigger. Unnaturally so.

'That's what they wanted, you know. They asked me to take them there.' He gestured around the circle with a hand. 'Here they are.'

Devitt swore he heard Reed growl.

'You're a murderer!' she snarled.

Devitt stepped in front of her again, worried she'd launch herself at the boy. Scare him off. Devitt was still trying to figure out how to get closer to arrest him. No doubt, this boy could run faster than him.

'You all mourn them like they were stolen,' Peter said lightly. 'But they gave themselves to me. They're the ones who did it.'

And Devitt's heart stilled. Ice slowly trickled through him at what this boy – no, a young adult now – was saying. What he truly believed. No matter what, Devitt had to act.

He took a slow step forwards. Just one, and then a second. Lazily, pulling his hat off and brushing it down lightly and trying to look casual. 'Assisted murder or murder through persuasion is still murder,' Devitt said, trying to match Peter's calm as he slowly stepped forwards.

But it was like trying to walk up to a sparrow without startling it off. Nearly impossible. Even as he focused on looking at his hat, from the corner of his eye he saw Peter twitch. Watching.

'A crime,' Devitt continued, firmer this time.

But as soon as he said that, Peter acted like Devitt didn't even exist. His eyes skirted past him, focus entirely on Reed.

'You came back to me,' he sang. 'I thought you would. I've missed you a few times, haven't I?'

Devitt hated that high-pitched sing-song voice, like the boy thought he was something innocent. Holy, even.

Then the boy stepped out of the circle and walked towards them – no, towards Reed. His eyes entirely locked on her.

He walked past Devitt without even a glance his way, and Devitt cursed that he'd tried to move closer to Peter, leaving Reed alone. Cursed that he should've told her to stay close.

'Names are such lovely gifts,' the boy said.

When Devitt tried to step between them again and grab the boy, Peter skipped around behind her with the ease of a young deer.

Peter reached out a slender arm, and no matter how much Reed seemed to draw back, his long, pale fingers managed to grab at her jaw and hold her in place. He leant his face in close to hers, smiling still. 'Are you ready now to give yours to me? Just for safe keeping?'

Devitt grabbed at Peter's arm. Tried to pull him off. But the boy was deceptively strong. Until Reed growled and lashed out, kicking and smacking, and the boy leapt back lightly, laughing.

'Get away from her.' Devitt stepped in front of the young girl again. 'You're dealing with me tonight.'

Peter laughed. 'Oh, the blind detective.' He danced back into his circle. 'But I don't want your name. You're too old. You already grew up.'

And then the boy's icy gaze froze further.

'Neverland won't take the ones who grew up.'

Devitt rose a brow. Nodded at the boy. 'Oh? And what about you?' he asked. 'Bit old to call yourself a boy now, aren't you? You're, what? Part your coming-of-age year, surely? Nineteen? Twenty?'

The boy looked shocked. Touched his hand to his heart. 'Never, detective. I never grew up. Isn't that the dream?'

His voice was soft – as if rot had overtaken it – and his smile just as so.

And then Peter gestured around them. 'Just like these lovely children. My lost ones. They'll never grow up either.'

'You're sick!' Reed tugged at Devitt's sleeve. 'Come on, Devitt. What are you waiting for? Weren't we taking him in?'

Devitt ignored her glare that he could feel piercing just below his shoulder. He certainly wanted to arrest Peter. More than anything. But he was curious to know why. Why the boy was doing this. Wanted to know more. And something was telling him that it was now or never.

That if he took the boy in now, he'd never speak again.

Here, he was bold.

'Oh, pretty thing,' Peter sighed, looking with corpse-eyed sympathy past him at Reed. 'You're just angry at me because I forgot to tell you how well-cared for your friend is.'

Devitt felt Reed stiffen, her grip clawing harder at where she'd grabbed his arm. They both watched as Peter glided about the circle, his footsteps barely audible. The boy bent in front of a skull on the outer line. Picked it up and stroked it.

'Here,' he said peacefully, admiring the bone carefully. 'She's doing excellently.' Then he looked across at Reed like he was simply checking the condition of fruit at a market. 'How many years has it been?'

Devitt looked back at Reed. The horror on her face twisted to anger.

'That's enough.' Devitt shot his arm out to block Reed from launching herself at him like a wild street cat and then shot Peter a scowl. 'This is the end of your game. You're coming back to the station for imprisonment on grounds of serial murder.'

No waiting now. Who cared what the boy said. He'd get the lads back in the prisons to draw it out of him – no matter how.

But the boy ignored him. Just bent down and replaced the skull on the line again.

'You *will* listen, Peter Cray,' Reed spat.

Only then did Peter pay attention. Stared up at them from where he crouched on the circle of bones.

'No,' he whispered, eyes flaring wide.

'Yes,' Devitt said, his heart pounding with conviction. 'You've haunted London's streets for too long, Peter Cray. Tonight is your last.'

But the boy still didn't look at Devitt. He rose to standing, eyes darting to Reed as if she'd betrayed him. He staggered, holding his head as if it would burst.

Peter moaned out as if in pain, stumbling back. 'You weren't supposed to remember.'

'You think I wouldn't write it down?' Reed said.

Devitt tried to push her back again. Didn't trust this boy not to do anything radical.

'You can write?' Peter shot her a wounded look, his voice high-pitched, broken, and weak.

'You think she'd be let into the station if she couldn't?' Devitt asked, feeling the need to defend her, though even he couldn't remember when or how she'd entered the force. It was almost like she'd just slipped in, made herself useful, and stayed.

And only then did Peter look at him.

The boy's dreamlike face soured. 'No,' he snarled. 'No, it doesn't work like this.' His corpse-pale eyes widened. 'This is not how it works!'

He took a step back, and Devitt launched himself towards him.

'But the rules ...' the boy started, before he noticed Devitt and horror flashed across his face.

The atmosphere in the warehouse smashed, like a glass window breaking in. And when it did, a fog rolled in like river water breaking the banks, only thick and grey and white.

Towards Peter.

And Peter Cray – with a face like a child who'd lost a game and was ready to have a tantrum over it – stepped back into the fog before Devitt could even reach him.

No.

Alice's white, tear-stained face flickered to memory. The street musician boy's face, peaceful and smiling as he lay twisted and broken, his accordion broken by his side.

It was all too much. Too much to lose.

'Cray!' Devitt bellowed, lunging with all his strength and reaching with outstretched fingers.

The fog was so thick it blinded him. But Peter had been *just there*. He knew it.

And so the blind detective reached.

Fabric and cool skin brushed his fingertips ...

... and then flitted away.

Devitt's heart hollowed, and in the white, he heard his own heartbeat echoing somewhere else.

'You still believe in doors, don't you?' a sing-song voice chided beyond the fog, echoing around the giant shell of the warehouse. 'Silly thing. Not everything needs a door to come in. Or leave.'

And then the fog washed back in on itself as instantly as it arrived, and Peter Cray was nowhere to be seen.

Devitt whirled on the spot. Looked back at Reed, hoping beyond anything she'd seen what had happened. But her face looked just as shocked, and her arms flailed out in a helpless shrug.

No.

A silence far too heavy to be natural fell, and ahead of them, at the centre of the circle of bones, a feather drifted to the floor.

No.

Devitt fell to his knees and screamed out with a frustration that clawed into his soul. So much he raked his nails painfully through his hair and stared at the damned feather as if it was to blame.

He'd grasped him.

He *had* gasped him, hadn't he?

So how ...?

Devitt bent forwards and slammed his fists into the warehouse floor with another cry. Years of frustration bubbling up, finally, at how unfair this dark world was.

But nothing so dark or unfair as missing the boy who built a faerie circle out of children's bones and then smiled.

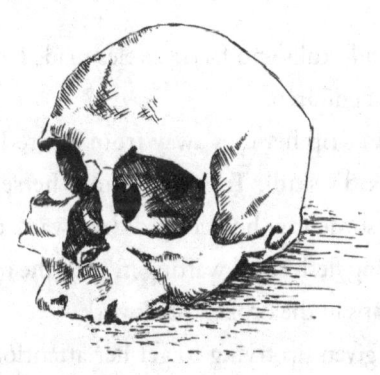

15

Among Forgotten Bones

Reed

Feathers and skulls and faerie circles made from the bones of the lost children.

Reed couldn't rip her eyes away from where Peter had put down her friend's skull. Tried to remind herself to breathe because now somehow her body didn't want to, especially with that rotting flesh smell wafting in with the midnight chill through the gaps in the broken brickwork.

Devitt had given up trying to get her attention. Called her name a few times. Tried to make sure she was okay. But what could she say after that?

And he must have known.

Now, he was striding around that damned circle of bones, probably getting as much information as he could while he waited for the police teams he'd sent for.

Reed was sure she should be taking notes. Learning from him. But she couldn't persuade her body to move.

Not since Peter had left in a cloud of fog like he was a fae king who could control weather.

Impossible, surely? For fog to take a human away.

A shaky breath wheezed past her still-chapped lips. That burning sensation returned as her mind caught up with her body.

That Peter Cray had touched her lips. Touched her lips with the same hands and the same strange gentleness that he'd touched these bones.

Her body shook with a zap of disgust that finally helped unlock her from her frozen horror, and Reed squealed and rubbed her lips on the back of her sleeve. It earned a concerned glance and shout from Devitt across the room, but she shrugged him off.

As if he could ever understand.

She paused as a pang of guilt poked at her stomach, and she glanced across at him. His own daughter nearly ended up here, like this.

Maybe, of all people, Devitt would be one of the few who could ever understand.

Reed told herself she'd go to join him. Help out. Be useful. Not just stand here moping and getting in the way. But just as she was convincing her shock-heavy legs to move, half the coppers in London barged through that screaming, broken door, their footsteps almost as loud as half the machines here would have been back when it was operational.

In no time, they'd flooded the floor, all shouting over one another as Devitt tried to control the chaos and bring some kind of order to the clear up. Barked at people not to disturb the bones.

Not that it would be easy. Not properly documenting and cleaning up a faerie circle of children's bones. The explanation of what had actually happened alone would take time enough.

And then it all became too much. The noise of the men in their fancy uniforms, bumbling and barging after the eerie fae silence, sent Reed's heart racing. Her body heated so rapidly she knew the next moment would empty everything from her stomach onto the floor.

Which could only be outside where no one here would know so she wouldn't be seen as the damned girl who threw up on the job. They'd claim they *knew* this would happen and would never let a woman enter the station again.

And so she somehow stumbled outside where the cold air hit her almost like she'd fallen into the Thames, and her body crashed.

Fell to her hands and knees and lost what little contents in her stomach she had to the frost-bitten mud.

She squeezed her eyes shut. Tried to convince herself to get up and go back in. Help out. Be useful. Keep this job she'd somehow fooled them into giving her just by sheer will and hanging around until they forgot she wasn't meant to be there.

But when old friend's skulls in soft, pale hands and fog rolling over circles of bones cloud your mind, every inch of good judgement disappears.

So Reed pulled herself up. Wiped her mouth on the back of her sleeve. And took one final glance at the worn-down old warehouse.

Imagined a feather floating slowly to the floor.

And turned her back on it, stepping into the midnight mist and heading for the safety of her crowded shared room.

16

After the Circle Closes

Devitt

M artha hadn't said anything when Devitt finally stepped through the door the next morning, grey and heavy and silent. She'd simply wrapped her arms around him, ushered him further inside, and led him to the kitchen.

The kids were already up. Alice sat feeding the toddler, and both squealed with delight as he stepped through the door.

His heart nearly burst, and it took every inch of his strength not to burst into tears.

At their love and joy. At their being here. Being alive.

How Alice had been saved and not ended up another mark on that damned circle.

Devitt couldn't bring himself to say anything. Just collapsed into a chair and watched as the three bustled about him, rushing up to give him hugs and kisses now and then. Giggles when his emotions got too much and he grabbed them back and hugged them so hard they squealed, and more so when he rubbed his bristly cheeks against theirs.

Normal life he'd so desperately needed amongst that disturbing mess. Especially after having spent the rest of the night pacing the old warehouse, looking at one too many children's empty eye sockets.

Not to mention discovering some children who must've died just before the Beechworth children, their bodies in various states of decomposition at the corner of that main hall. The cause of the smell.

Tragic.

Had it not been for the Beechworth kids causing attention, Devitt wondered how much longer this would have gone on for. How many children would have been taken unnoticed.

And now he understood Reed's rage at street kids going forgotten.

All those children whose bones made that circle …

Devitt blinked back to the moment. Made himself pretend everything was alright, just for a while. Before he had to go back to the station and start reporting. Cataloguing children's bones and digging through old birth reports and missing people notes.

So Peter Cray was gone, but Devitt knew better than to think this was the end. As he chugged the last of his tea and watched Martha brush Alice's long yellow hair and tie braids with lovely green ribbons he'd bought her for her birthday a few months ago, his heart stuttered once again to remember how close they'd been to losing Alice.

And to wonder whether Peter would come back here for revenge.

But another part of him sensed that boy was long gone by now. Ready to try again somewhere else. But it was for that reason Devitt was determined to do his best to report what he knew. Document it so if need arose in the future, they'd be ready. And then they could spread the news to every city in England.

He was back at the station in no time. Sleep deprived and grumbling about having to stoop for hours over a desk in a room with poor lighting, and a window that let in more cold air than grimy light.

Except, there was one change.

A girl in a giant new coat stood to attention by his desk as he entered.

He paused. Cocked his head to the side.

'Promotion suits you,' Devitt said, placing his own hat on his desk as he walked past her.

Reed turned as he sat down and grinned at him.

'They said this was all they had on hand,' she said, fiddling with the lapels and buttons on her new station-issued uniform.

Officially a constable.

Devitt let out a snort. 'It looks like it's about to swallow you.'

'I'll grow into it!' she objected, but stuffed her hands into her pockets like she always did and shrugged up her shoulders.

'What, in seven years when you're finally an adult?' he said quietly after quickly leaning around to make sure no one would be able to overhear.

She puffed up her chest. 'Two! And anyway, this is way cosier. Will keep the cold air off more.'

Devitt supposed that bit at least might be right.

'And it makes me look bigger. More intimidating,' she continued.

Devitt couldn't help the chuckle that burst from his lips. 'If you say so.' Didn't have the heart to tell her she looked more like when a child tries on their parents' clothes.

Her brows rose like they always did when she was about to start bickering, so Devitt shuffled in his seat and deflected.

'So,' he started, suddenly not sure on how to put it.

She'd disappeared last night. After Cray had. After Scotland Yard had arrived. And now she was here acting as if nothing had happened, which was more concerning than if she'd arrived looking like a ghost.

He fiddled with the papers on his desk. Glanced up at her. 'You okay?'

She stiffened – as expected – and all fight washed from her face in an instant. 'Yeah,' she said in such a low voice he barely caught it. She sniffed then met his gaze hesitantly. 'You?'

Devitt let out a long exhale. 'Yeah.' And then the silence weighed so heavily that it almost called back to the night before in the warehouse.

'Well,' he said, clearing his throat. 'Better hop to it. You saw how much paperwork we've got.'

Lost children don't identify themselves, he added to himself.

Reed straightened and saluted like she'd no doubt seen all the other constables do, clicking her heels smartly together.

'And it looks like you get to move your desk away from that tiny hole in the cabinets,' he added. She shot him a confused frown. 'Commissioner thinks I'm out of my mind to hire a young woman onto the force,' he explained. 'So you're under my supervision. On my head if anything goes wrong.'

He sent her a warning look.

'Don't let me down.'

She grinned. Saluted again and ran off to get her desk while Devitt picked up a lead pencil and stared at a blank leaf of paper, wondering how the hell he was meant to write a letter to explain all this to the other police forces across England.

Because how did one seriously write about chalk stars and bird bones and feathers and children who jumped to their own deaths with smiles on their faces to the lilting sound of a pan pipe lullaby? For a boy who thought he was a fae king and had disappeared in a breath of fog?

You couldn't. But they had to. In case it started happening again. In case that boy came back.

And in case someone else picked up a feather and sang that heart-chillingly haunting song.

Epilogue

It was just a dark backstreet in Sheffield. An alley no one really paid much attention to.

The night was dark and a light, icy misting rain fell unendingly, soaking through clothes in minutes.

A brick wall stood behind the old butcher's shop – now closed for the night. There, in white chalk and dust, a boy, humming a haunting song only he seemed to know, scratched out a perfect crescent moon and two stars to the right of it. And within the second star, he drew a smile.

Circled the star.

Then, still humming, he turned away. Dropped the chalk on the street floor and brushed down his hands before taking a feather from his pocket.

And threw it above himself in the air.

It drifted slowly to the floor as he dashed away.

About Sarah Caelan

Hey everyone, and thanks for being here.

I'm Sarah Caelan, previously writing as Sarah Kate Ishii. As of releasing this book, I'm 32 years old, and my life has been full of adventures, real and fictional. I met my husband during my time living in Japan, and now we live in Australia with our energetic and spirited toddler.

Other than writing, of course, I love hanging out with my friends and family, being outside, walking, working out, daydreaming as I listen to music, and getting back into art and drawing.

Ever since I was young, I've been completely enchanted by books. Especially fantasy books. I grew up immersing myself in books like *The Worst Witch*, *The Edge Chronicles*, *His Dark Materials*, and *Sabriel*. As I got older, I discovered Robin Hobb's *The Liveship Traders*, a series that utterly captivated me with its grand storytelling and deeply human characters. Books like these (and anime, manga, and Studio Ghibli) made me wish I could just BE IN the story and inspired me to write too.

Books weren't just entertainment for me. As a child, I was often unwell and couldn't go out much, so stories became my adventures, and characters became my friends. Sounds super nerdy to put it like that, but those pages gave me another world and another life to live in. I could be whoever I wanted, without illness. (Often with the magical powers we all secretly dream about, right?)

It's this same experience I want to give my readers: the joy of being completely immersed in a story, to the point where the real world fades away and you feel like you ARE a part of the story. The best feeling.

I also wanted to share something really cool.

This book, that I fondly just call *Feather*, is a milestone for me because it's the first book I've illustrated myself.

When I was a child, I grew up insisting I was going to be an author-artist. (It always came as the pair!) But life happened, as it does, and study and uni and work get in the way and you have to drop a few balls to ensure the important ones don't break.

Art got dropped. Writing was eventually picked back up again.

But that side of me that loved drawing and painting remained hidden (and, frankly, a little sulky), until I finally gave myself the space to draw even just a few minutes each day. Probably after some New Years resolution. And honestly, keeping it daily and consistent was tough, so I just made sure I did it as much as I could spare.

#MamaLife

Then, because my art style always leant more to the gothic when I was a student, a little voice at the back of my head told me *Feather* would be the perfect book to start adding little vibe images. Readers at cons and markets often talked with me about how cool it would be for books to have the occasional illustration again like the books we read as kids, and I found myself thinking 'why not try'.

And because I'm really big on people chasing their curiosity and making sure to fit in time for things that bring them joy, I knew I had to act on what I'd said all those years ago as a child.

So maybe one day I can still be that author-artist I dreamt of back then. Until then, I hope you'll start seeing more of my sketches appearing, just like here.

And I had so much fun drawing them. Especially the mushroom faerie circles. Don't the mushrooms look like cute little ladies!

'Well, hello there.'

Also by Sarah

If you enjoyed reading *Feather*, I'd love if you tried:

And before I wrote under Sarah Caelan,
I wrote as Sarah Kate Ishii.

Book 1

Book 2

Book 3 will be coming soon!